The End of America

America Series, Volume 1

William Myers

Published by William Myers, 2024.

THE END OF AMERICA

First edition. August 17, 2024.

ISBN: 979-8227512314

Written by William Myers.

I dedicate this book to our conservative politicians who pray for the nation to return to its old glory.

THE END OF AMERICA

Foreword

The Sovereignty of God over the Nations
Introduction

CONCLUSION

Foreword
The Sovereignty of God over the Nations

In the beginning, God created the heavens and the earth, and from that moment, His hand has guided the course of history. As it is written, "The earth is the Lord's, and everything in it, the world, and all who live in it" (Psalm 24:1). Borders or boundaries do not limit his sovereignty, for He is the Creator and Sustainer of all things.

Nations rise and fall according to His will, as the prophet Daniel declared, "He changes times and seasons; He deposes kings and raises up others" (Daniel 2:21). Throughout history, empires have come and gone, but it is God who holds the ultimate authority. The rulers of this world may boast of their power, but they are mere instruments in the hands of the Almighty. "The king's heart is in the hand of the Lord; He directs it like a watercourse wherever He pleases" (Proverbs 21:1).

When Israel faced the might of Babylon, the Lord allowed the Babylonian Empire to rise, using it as a tool of judgment. Yet even in their captivity, God's people were reminded of His supremacy. Through the prophet Jeremiah, God said, "I made the earth, and the people and animals that are on the earth, by My great power and outstretched arm, and I give it to anyone I please" (Jeremiah 27:5). The rise of Babylon was not by chance, but by divine decree, showing that even the greatest of powers are subject to His will.

But God's rule is not one of tyranny or caprice. It is rooted in righteousness and justice. As it is written, "Righteousness and justice are the foundation of Your throne; love and faithfulness go before You" (Psalm 89:14). His judgments are true, and His rule is marked by compassion for the oppressed and a hatred of evil. "The Lord reigns forever; He has established His throne for judgment. He rules the world in righteousness and judges the peoples with equity" (Psalm 9:7-8).

In the New Testament, the apostle Paul echoes this truth, affirming that God is sovereign over all nations, even those that do not acknowledge Him. He tells the Athenians, "From one man He made all the nations, that they should inhabit the whole earth; and He marked out their appointed times in history and the boundaries of their lands" (Acts 17:26). This divine orchestration underscores the truth that God is the ultimate ruler of history, guiding the destinies of nations according to His purposes.

Yet, in His sovereignty, God also calls nations to account. He warns through the prophet Isaiah, "Woe to those who enact evil statutes and to those who constantly record unjust decisions" (Isaiah 10:1). The nations that pursue wickedness, injustice, and idolatry will not escape His judgment. "Behold, the nations are like a drop from a bucket, and are regarded as a speck of dust on the scales" (Isaiah 40:15). God's power is incomparable, and His authority over the nations is absolute.

The ultimate display of God's rule over the nations is seen in the coming of His Son, Jesus Christ. In Revelation, the apostle John sees a future vision, where Christ is revealed as the King of kings and Lord of lords. "With justice He and wages war. His eyes are like blazing fire, and on His head are many crowns... On His robe and His thigh He has this name written: King of kings and Lord of lords" (Revelation 19:11-16). In this vision, all nations and kings bow before Him, acknowledging His supreme authority.

As the nation rages and the people plot in vain, God remains unshaken, laughing at their futile schemes. "The One enthroned in heaven laughs; the Lord scoffs at them. He rebukes them in His anger and terrifies them in His wrath, saying, 'I have installed My king on Zion, My holy mountain'" (Psalm 2:4-6). The final victory belongs to the Lord, and all nations will one day bow before His throne.

In the end, the Scriptures remind us that God governs the fate of nations. "The Lord Almighty has sworn, 'Surely, as I have planned so that it will be, and as I have purposed, so it will happen'" (Isaiah 14:24).

His plans cannot be thwarted, and His purposes will stand. As believers, we can rest in the knowledge that our God reigns and His kingdom is everlasting. "For dominion belongs to the Lord, and He rules over the nations" (Psalm 22:28).

Introduction

For centuries, America stood as a beacon of hope, a land forged in the fires of revolution and tempered by the principles of freedom, democracy, and unwavering faith in God. Our founding fathers, guided by divine providence, crafted a nation where liberty was not just a right but a sacred duty. It was a country where the pursuit of happiness was intertwined with a moral compass rooted in the eternal truths of scripture. For generations, this great experiment in self-governance thrived, growing into a global superpower, a shining city on a hill.

Yet, like all empires before us, the seeds of our downfall were sown not by external enemies, but from within. As the years passed, a new ideology began to take root in the fertile soil of American society—an ideology that promised progress but delivered decay, that preached tolerance but fostered division. Liberal theology, with its seductive promises of a more inclusive and enlightened society, slowly eroded the moral fabric of our nation. It stripped away the foundational beliefs that had once united us, replacing them with a hollow creed of relativism and moral ambiguity.

Under the guise of compassion and modernity, the architects of this new order dismantled the very institutions that had made America great. They redefined liberty not as a gift from God but as a right granted by the state. They reinterpreted the Constitution not as a sacred covenant but as a malleable document, subject to the whims of popular opinion. They marginalized those who held fast to traditional values, labelling them as outdated, intolerant, or even dangerous.

In time, this shift in theology and management led to a nation adrift, unmoored from the principles that had once guided it. The consequences were catastrophic. As faith in God waned, so too did the moral resolve of the American people. Leaders, once guided by a sense of duty to their Creator and their countrymen, now governed by polls and public sentiment, their actions dictated by a desire to please rather than to do what was right.

Throughout the Bible, there are numerous instances where God used heathen nations as instruments of judgment against the Jewish people, mainly when they strayed from His commandments and worshiped other gods. This theme is evident in several key events in the Old Testament:

The Assyrian Captivity

In 722 B.C., the Assyrians conquered the northern kingdom of Israel. This occurred after the Israelites had repeatedly turned away from God, embracing idolatry and ignoring the prophets sent to warn them. God allowed the Assyrians, a powerful and ruthless empire, to invade and destroy Israel, scattering the ten tribes across the Assyrian Empire. This event is seen as divine punishment for Israel's disobedience.

The Babylonian Exile

In 586 B.C., the southern kingdom of Judah fell to the Babylonians. King Nebuchadnezzar captured Jerusalem, destroyed the Temple, and exiled the Jewish people to Babylon. This exile was a direct result of Judah's persistent idolatry and failure to follow God's laws despite the warnings of prophets like Jeremiah. The exile is one of the most significant events in Jewish history and is seen as a period of purification and reflection.

The Persian Conquest

While the Babylonians were used as instruments of punishment, the Persian Empire, under King Cyrus, was used as an instrument of restoration. In 539 B.C., Cyrus conquered Babylon, allowing the Jewish exiles to return to Jerusalem and rebuild the Temple. Though not a worshiper of the God of Israel, Cyrus is called God's "anointed" in Isaiah, showing that God can use even foreign rulers to fulfill His purposes.

The Roman Occupation

The Jewish people lived under Roman rule during Jesus's time. Although the Romans were not used in the same direct punitive manner as the Assyrians or Babylonians, their occupation of Israel and the eventual destruction of the Second Temple in A.D. 70 are often seen in the context of divine judgment, particularly as a result of the Jewish leadership's rejection of Jesus as the Messiah.

This book chronicles the fall of a nation—a tale of how America abandoned the very principles that had made it firm in its quest for progress. It is a story of how liberal theology and misguided management led to our national identity's erosion, our moral foundation's decay, and ultimately, the collapse of the American experiment.

But it is also a warning. For those who still believe in the America that was, who still hold dear the values of freedom, democracy, and faith, there is a lesson to be learned from our history. To prevent such a fall in the future, we must return to the principles that made us great. We must rekindle our faith in God, restore the moral compass that once guided our decisions, and reassert the timeless truths our founders knew were essential for a free and just society.

In these pages, you will find the story of a nation that lost its way and the hope that it can find its way back. For as long as some remember what America was meant to be, there is a chance for redemption, a chance to rebuild, and a chance to restore the great promise of this land. Even if overran, God can turn the tide to those who return to Him.

THE END OF A NATION

In the annals of history, great civilizations have risen and fallen, often in dramatic and cataclysmic events. Yet, some collapses occur not with a bang but with a whisper. Such was the fate of democracy in the United States of America in the early 21st century. The seeds of its downfall were sown long before the final collapse, nurtured by complacency, division, and external manipulation. As President Emily Perrin took office, she inherited a nation on the brink, unaware of the silent forces conspiring against the very foundation of democracy.

"It was Nikita Khrushchev who said that Russia would take America from within without firing a single shot." These words, spoken during the height of the Cold War, seemed prophetic as the events of the 2020s unfolded. Khrushchev, the shrewd Soviet Premier, understood that the true power of a nation lies not only in its military might but also in its ideological cohesion. The United States, with its robust democratic institutions and a populace that cherished freedom, seemed impregnable from without. However, from within, the cracks were beginning to show.

The early warnings were there for those who cared to see. Political polarization had reached unprecedented levels, with Americans divided along ideological, racial, and socioeconomic lines. Once hailed as a tool for democratizing information, social media became a battleground for misinformation and division. Foreign adversaries, recognizing the power of these platforms, exploited them to sow discord and distrust.

Economic inequality further exacerbated these tensions. The middle class, long the backbone of American democracy, became increasingly squeezed. Wealth concentrated in the hands of a few, while the rest struggled to make ends meet. This disparity bred resentment and fuelled the flames of populism as demagogues on both sides of the political spectrum capitalized on the public's discontent.

While America grappled with its internal divisions, external threats loomed large. Russia, under the leadership of President Vladimir Miskal, embarked on a campaign of hybrid warfare designed to undermine American democracy from within. Utilizing a combination of cyberattacks, propaganda, and covert operations, Russia sought to weaken the United States by exploiting its vulnerabilities.

China, too, played a role in this silent war. Under President Xi Jinping, China expanded its influence globally, challenging America's dominance on the world stage. Through economic coercion, cyber espionage, and strategic alliances, China aimed to create a new world order where democratic values took a backseat to authoritarianism.

As the United States struggled to maintain its democratic principles, authoritarianism rose globally. From Eastern Europe to South America, democratic backsliding became a troubling trend. Leaders who once championed democratic values increasingly embraced autocratic measures to maintain power.

The turning point came with the election of President Emily Perrin. Her victory, though a triumph for human rights and democratic values, also marked a period of intense challenge. President Perrin inherited a fractured nation, beset by internal and external pressures. Her administration's efforts to fortify NATO alliances and stand firm on human rights were met with fierce resistance, both domestically and internationally.

While principled, Perrin's presidency faced relentless opposition. The political climate grew increasingly toxic, with partisan battles overshadowing meaningful governance. Congress, paralyzed by gridlock, struggled to pass critical legislation. Meanwhile, foreign adversaries intensified their efforts, exploiting every weakness to further destabilize the nation.

As the silent collapse unfolded, the American people found themselves living in a state of constant uncertainty. Civil unrest became a common occurrence, with protests and counter-protests erupting regularly. The media, once a pillar of democracy, was mired in accusations of bias and fake news, further eroding public trust.

Economically, the country teetered on the edge. The wealth gap widened, and the middle class continued to shrink. Small businesses struggled to survive, while multinational corporations wielded unprecedented power. The American Dream, once a beacon of hope and opportunity, seemed increasingly out of reach for many.

The final blow came from a foreign invasion and external attacks on the infrastructure of government and large corporations—a series of events, seemingly unrelated but deeply interconnected, culminated in the collapse of American democracy.

Cyberattacks crippled critical infrastructure, causing widespread panic and chaos. Unable to unite in crisis, political leaders resorted to draconian measures to maintain order. Civil liberties were curtailed in the name of security, and the rule of law began to erode.

In the heart of Washington D.C., the once vibrant and bustling capital, a sense of foreboding hung heavy in the air. The institutions that had upheld democracy for centuries seemed fragile, their foundations weakened by years of neglect and assault. As President Perrin addressed the nation, her voice carried a mixture of resolve and despair. She knew that the America she had sworn to protect was on the brink of an unprecedented transformation.

As democracy faltered, a new era emerged. The fall of American democracy had far-reaching implications, reshaping the global order. Authoritarian regimes, emboldened by America's collapse, expanded their influence unabated. Once championed by the United States, the values of freedom and human rights were found to be defended less on the world stage.

Yet, amidst the darkness, there remained a glimmer of hope. The story of America's fall was not just one of defeat but also resilience. Across the nation, pockets of resistance formed, determined to reclaim the democratic ideals that had defined the country. These individuals, from all walks of life, understood that the fight for democracy was far from over.

The fall of democracy in the United States was a cautionary tale, a reminder of the fragility of freedom. It was a story of how a great nation could falter, beset by internal strife and external manipulation. But it was also a story of how, even in the darkest times, the spirit of democracy could endure, waiting for the moment to rise again.

It was during this period of unrest the great invasion took place. A war that did more than cripple a nation; it eliminated democracy and buried it in the sands of obscurity.

January 20, 2029

Emily Perrin stood on the steps of the Capitol, her hand on the Bible, taking the oath of office as the first woman president of the United States. Her victory had been historic, a triumph of progressive values and a promise of sweeping reforms. Her inaugural address was a call to action, emphasizing unity, social justice, and a renewed commitment to international cooperation.

Sadly, Emily took an oath on a Bible she did not honour, a God she would not worship. and a government she felt the need to corrupt. She represented everything terrible in America, but the liberal masses cheered her on.

Her presidency quickly became a lightning rod for international tensions. Her progressive policies, particularly her stance on abortion, the LGBTQ movement, and her plans to move America into socialism, would add to the downfall of the nation.

However, Emily's selection reverberated across the globe, stirring unease among confident world leaders who perceived her leadership as a potential threat to their ambitions.

The Kremlin, Moscow, Russia

President Miskal sat in his office, the dim light casting ominous shadows on the walls adorned with portraits of past Russian leaders. His keen eyes scanned the reports on his desk. Emily Perrin's victory had not been taken lightly. Her resolute stance on human rights and her intent to fortify NATO alliances were unmistakable challenges to Russian interests.

Miskal took a deep breath and picked up the secure phone on his desk, dialling a number he knew by heart. The call connected almost immediately.

"Xi, we need to discuss our mutual interests," Miskal said without preamble. "Perrin's presidency poses a significant threat to our strategic objectives."

Xi Jinping's voice came through the secure line with a calm, calculated tone. "Indeed, Miskal. Her policies are aimed at undermining our influence and expanding NATO's reach. We must act swiftly and decisively."

The two leaders had long shared a pragmatic alliance built on mutual benefit and a shared opposition to Western dominance. As Miskal and Xi discussed their options, they knew the stakes had never been higher. Perrin's administration had already begun consolidating support among European allies. It was making overtures to countries in the Indo-Pacific region, seeking to encircle Russia and China with a web of alliances.

"We need a distraction," Miskal mused. "Something that will force her to spread her forces thin, something that will divide her attention. "Xi nodded, though Miskal couldn't see it. "Agreed. A confrontation would be too risky, but we can create enough chaos to destabilize her position."

Miskal leaned back in his chair, the gears in his mind turning rapidly. "I have an idea. What if we stage large-scale military exercises near the Alaskan border? The Americans will be forced to divert significant resources to their northernmost state."

Xi's eyes narrowed in thought. "And while they are preoccupied with defending Alaska, we can pursue our interests elsewhere. It could work, but it must be executed flawlessly."

Miskal smiled cold and calculating. "Leave that to me. I'll begin the preparations immediately. In the meantime, we must ensure our other plans are in motion. Everything must be synchronized in the South China Sea, Eastern Europe, cyber operations."

As Miskal and Xi finalized their plans, operatives on both sides moved into action. In Moscow, General Viktor Sokolov was summoned to the Kremlin. A veteran strategist with a ruthless reputation, Sokolov was briefed on Operation "BEAR" and requested that the Alaskan invasion be identified as the "Northern Blizzard." He listened intently as Miskal outlined the plan, his mind already calculating the logistics and tactical maneuvers required.

"General, this operation must be executed with precision. The goal is not a full-scale invasion but to create the appearance of one. We need the Americans to believe that we are preparing to invade Alaska. This will force them to divert their attention and resources."

Sokolov nodded. "Understood, President Miskal. I'll ensure that our forces are ready. The exercises will be massive and highly visible."

Meanwhile, similar preparations were underway in Beijing. Chinese cyber units, some of the most advanced in the world, began coordinating with their Russian counterparts. Their mission was to launch a series of cyberattacks that would sow confusion and disrupt communications in the U.S. Simultaneously, Chinese naval forces increased their presence in the South China Sea, conducting drills and maneuvers that signaled a potential escalation.

Pyongyang, North Korea

Supreme Leader Kim Jong-un received the encrypted messages from Moscow and Beijing with curiosity and caution. North Korea's position was always precarious, but the prospect of coordinated action with Russia and China was intriguing. Perrin's firm stance against nuclear proliferation and her commitment to South Korea's defense were direct challenges to his regime.

Kim called for an urgent meeting with his top generals. "We must be prepared for all ambitions do not jeopardize our sovereignty."

Washington, D.C., United States

Unaware of the storm, President Perrin immersed herself in her new role. Her inauguration speech had been a rallying cry for unity and progress. She had already begun working on initiatives to strengthen international alliances, improve domestic infrastructure, and champion environmental sustainability.

But intelligence reports started trickling in, hinting at unusual communications between Russia, China, and North Korea. The National Security Advisor, Richard Harris, briefed Perrin on the potential threats.

"Madam President, we have reason to believe that our adversaries are coordinating efforts against us," Harris said, his expression grave. "We must bolster our defenses and with our allies immediately." Emily sighed and responded, *"Our allies have elected to remain neutral."*

The look on the faces of the Pentagon officials was heart-wrenching. These individuals knew that America, with her two million soldiers, would have little impact if these three superpowers incurred an invasion. That was an estimate of over twenty million enemy soldiers crossing our borders.

A Remote Base in Siberia

Russian, Chinese, and North Korean military officials gathered secretly, finalizing their plans. The operation, codenamed "Iron Veil," aimed to destabilize the United States through cyberattacks, economic sabotage, military posturing, and then a full invasion. "We strike in unison," Miskal declared, his voice echoing in the cold, austere room. "Our strength lies in our coordination. Perrin will not see this coming."

Operation Iron Veil: The Detailed Plan

The Kremlin, Moscow, Russia

The room was dimly lit, a cold, austere space where Russian, Chinese, and North Korean military officials gathered. General Miskal, a seasoned strategist from the Russian army, stood before a large map of the United States, illuminated by a single overhead light. His counterparts, General Zhang Wei of China and General Kim Hyun of North Korea listened intently as Miskal outlined the final stages of Operation Iron Veil.

Phase 1: Cyber Warfare and Economic Sabotage'

The operation began with a coordinated cyber assault aimed at crippling the United States' critical infrastructure and economy.

Cyber Warfare

Power Grids: Russian cyber units would target the Eastern and Western Interconnections of the U.S. power grid, causing widespread blackouts in major cities such as New York, Los Angeles, Chicago, and Houston.

Financial Sector: Chinese hackers would infiltrate major financial institutions, including the Federal Reserve, JPMorgan Chase, and Goldman Sachs. The attacks would freeze transactions, corrupt data, and create panic in the stock markets.

Communication Networks: North Korean cyber operatives would disrupt telecommunications networks, targeting AT&T, Verizon, and critical internet service providers to create chaos and hinder emergency responses.

Economic Sabotage

1. **Stock Market Crash:** Simultaneous cyberattacks would cause a catastrophic crash in the New York Stock Exchange, wiping out trillions in value and leading to an economic meltdown.
2. **Supply Chain Disruptions:** Chinese operatives would sabotage key ports in Los Angeles and Long Beach, disrupting the flow of goods and creating shortages nationwide.
3. **Phase 2: Military Posturing and Deception**

While the United States grappled with the chaos from the initial phase, the three nations would use military posturing to distract and spread U.S. forces thin.

Military Posturing

Russia: Would conduct large-scale military exercises near the Alaskan border, simulating an imminent invasion. This would force the U.S. to divert significant resources to its northernmost state.

Russian Military Exercises Near Alaska

Objectives

Russia's decision to conduct large-scale military exercises near the Alaskan border aims to achieve several objectives:

1. Diversion of U.S. Resources: By simulating an imminent invasion, Russia forces the U.S. to divert significant military resources to its northernmost state, weakening its ability to respond to threats elsewhere.

2. Psychological Warfare: The presence of a large Russian military force near Alaska can cause public fear and uncertainty, undermining confidence in the U.S. government's ability to protect its territory.

3. Testing U.S. Response: These exercises allow Russia to observe and analyse U.S. military response strategies and capabilities, providing valuable intelligence for future operations.

4. Execution

The exercises involve various branches of the Russian military, ground troops, naval forces, and the air force. The operations simulate amphibious landings, air assaults, and defensive maneuvers. Advanced weaponry and equipment, such as fighter jets, bombers, submarines, and electronic warfare systems, are prominently featured.

U.S. Response

In response to the perceived threat, the U.S. would likely implement several measures:

1. **Force Deployment:** Redeployment of military assets, including fighter jets, bombers, and naval vessels, to Alaska and nearby regions.
2. **Joint**
3. **Exercises:** Increased joint military exercises with NATO allies in the Arctic and North Pacific regions to demonstrate resolve and readiness.
4. **Intelligence Gathering:** Enhanced surveillance and intelligence-gathering activities to monitor Russian movements and intentions.

Strain on Military Resources

The diversion of U.S. military resources to Alaska can strain its ability to respond to other global threats. With significant assets tied up in the north, the U.S. may struggle to address simultaneous crises in the Asia-Pacific, Europe, or the Middle East.

Operation Iron Veil: The Espionage Prelude

The Kremlin, Moscow, Russia

President Miskal sat with his top intelligence advisors in the heart of the Kremlin. The conversation was focused and tense. The plan for the military invasion was already in motion, but Miskal knew that to ensure its success, it needed to weaken America from within. The SVR, Russia's foreign intelligence service, was tasked with this critical mission.

"Activate our sleeper cells," Miskal ordered. "We must sow discord and confusion. Our allies in Beijing and Pyongyang will do the same. This will be a coordinated effort."

Pyongyang, North Korea

Supreme Leader Kim Jong-un convened his top intelligence officials and directed them to collaborate with their Russian and Chinese counterparts. The Reconnaissance General Bureau (RGB), North Korea's primary intelligence agency, would be crucial in the upcoming espionage efforts. "We will strike at their heart," Kim declared. "Our allies are depending on us. This is our chance to reshape the world order."

Beijing, China

In a similarly secretive meeting, President Xi Jinping met with the heads of the Ministry of

State Security (MSS). They discussed the various fronts of their espionage campaign, which included cyberattacks on American infrastructure and manipulating social media to spread misinformation and division. "Ensure our assets in the U.S. are prepared," Xi said firmly. "Our goal is to create internal chaos that will divert their attention from our military maneuvers."

Washington D. C.

Unbeknownst to President Perrin, a silent war had already begun. SVR operatives embedded in various parts of American society activated, receiving coded instructions through seemingly innocuous messages. MSS agents intensified their cyber operations, targeting power grids, financial institutions, and critical infrastructure. Meanwhile, RGB operatives focused on espionage and sabotage, preparing to strike vital military installations.

The coordinated efforts of these three influential spy organizations aimed to destabilize the United States, making it more vulnerable to the impending military invasion.

A Secret Base in Virginia

Emily Perrin's administration, through its counterintelligence efforts, had detected an unusual increase in cyber activity and minor incidents of sabotage. At the FBI's Cyber Division headquarters, analysts worked around the clock to identify the sources of these threats.

"Madam President," Richard Harris, the National Security Advisor, briefed Perrin in the Situation Room. We have confirmed that Russia,

China, and North Korea are coordinating an espionage effort. Their goal appears to be to destabilize us from within."

President Perrin listened intently, her mind racing through the possibilities. "We need to counter this immediately. Strengthen our cybersecurity, tighten security around critical infrastructure, and deploy counter-espionage measures. Inform our allies and get their support." Sadly, when the American president reached out to the various allies, they unanimously declined.

New York City, New York

An SVR sleeper agent, known only as Dmitri, received his final instructions at a seemingly ordinary office building. His mission was to disrupt the financial sector, causing panic and confusion. Dmitri and other agents initiated a series of attacks on central banks and stock exchanges, causing brief but significant disruptions.

Silicon Valley, California

MSS operatives infiltrated tech companies, stealing sensitive data and planting malware. Their goal was to cripple communication networks and cause widespread fear among the populace.

Los Angeles, California

RGB agents focused on military installations. Using a network of local sympathizers and covert operations, they managed to sabotage a critical supply depot, causing significant logistical challenges for the U.S. military.

The coordinated efforts of the Russian, Chinese, and North Korean intelligence divisions created a plan they identified as Code Name BEAR (Banks, Elections, Airways, Retaliation).

Code Name BEAR: The Strategic Espionage Plan

1. Banks

The first phase of Operation BEAR focused on the financial sector. The objective was to destabilize the American economy by targeting its banking infrastructure. This phase involved:

- **Cyberattacks:** Coordinated cyberattacks on major banks, financial institutions, and stock exchanges to cause system failures, data breaches, and unauthorized fund transfers. This aimed to create chaos, erode public trust in the financial system, and disrupt the economy.
- **Physical Sabotage:** Covert operatives infiltrated critical financial hubs and conducted physical sabotage, such as tampering with ATMs, disrupting communication lines, and causing localized power outages. These actions were designed to amplify the impact of the cyberattacks and create widespread panic.

2. Elections

This phase targeted the democratic process, aiming to undermine the legitimacy of the U.S. government and sow discord among the population. This phase involved:

- **Election Interference:** Cyber operatives hacked into voter databases, altering voter information and registration data. They also attempted to breach electronic voting systems to manipulate results and create confusion on Election Day.
- **Disinformation Campaigns:** Using social media platforms,

the operatives spread false information, conspiracy theories, and inflammatory content to polarize voters, incite civil unrest, and delegitimize the electoral process. This included targeting key swing states and demographics to influence public opinion and voter behavior.

3. Airways

The third phase focused on disrupting the transportation and communication networks, particularly the aviation sector. This phase involved:

- **Cyberattacks on Air Traffic Control Systems:** MSS hackers targeted air traffic control and airline reservation systems, causing flight delays, cancellations, and potential safety risks. The goal was to paralyze air travel, create logistical nightmares, and undermine public confidence in transportation safety.
- **Physical Attacks on Key Airports:** RGB agents planned physical attacks on major airports, including sabotage of critical infrastructure and potential terrorist activities. These attacks aimed to cause mass casualties, instill fear, and further disrupt the transportation network.

4. Retaliation

The final phase, Retaliation, was a contingency plan to respond to any U.S. countermeasures and to maintain pressure on the American government. This phase involved:

- **Covert Operations:** SVR, MSS, and RGB operatives prepared to execute a series of covert operations, including assassinations, kidnappings, and bombings, targeting key political figures, military leaders, and infrastructure. These actions were designed to retaliate against any U.S. attempts to counteract the espionage efforts and to keep the U.S. government off balance.

- **Prolonged Cyber Warfare:** Continued cyberattacks on critical infrastructure, including power grids, water supply systems, and healthcare networks, to maintain a state of perpetual crisis and hinder recovery efforts. The objective was to exhaust American resources and morale.

Implementation and Coordination

Operation BEAR's success relied on seamless coordination between the SVR, MSS, and RGB. Intelligence sharing, joint planning sessions, and synchronized execution were critical to the plan's effectiveness. Special task forces were created to oversee each phase, ensuring that actions were carried out simultaneously and precisely.

The Silent Infiltration

While the American people rallied to defend their nation against overt military aggression, another, more insidious threat lurked in the shadows. For years, Russia, China, and North Korea had been meticulously planting spies within the United States, weaving a complex web of espionage aimed at undermining American security and sowing discord.

These spies were not the cloak-and-dagger operatives of old but sophisticated agents embedded in every facet of American society. From corporate boardrooms to research labs, military installations to political offices, their presence was pervasive, their motives concealed beneath layers of deception.

The Russian Strategy

With its long history of espionage dating back to the Cold War, Russia utilized a multi-faceted approach. The SVR (Foreign Intelligence Service) and GRU (Military Intelligence) spearheaded operations to gather critical information, influence public opinion, and sabotage key infrastructure.

Russian operatives infiltrated American tech companies, gaining access to cutting-edge research and development projects. They hacked into corporate networks, stealing trade secrets and intellectual property, which they then used to bolster Russian technological advancements and disrupt American economic superiority.

In addition to cyber-espionage, Russia employed "illegals" — highly trained agents living under deep cover. These operatives built seemingly ordinary lives, often residing in the U.S. for decades, integrating into communities and establishing influential positions. They aimed to gather intelligence, recruit assets, and subtly influence political processes.

One such operative, known only by his code name, "Vladimir," had successfully infiltrated a principal defense contractor. For years, he funnelled sensitive information about American weapons systems back to Moscow, providing Russia with a strategic advantage and compromising U.S. national security.

The Chinese Network

China's espionage efforts were equally sophisticated and pervasive. The Ministry of State Security (MSS) orchestrated a vast network of spies and informants, focusing on traditional and cyber espionage.

Chinese agents targeted American universities and research institutions, exploiting the open and collaborative nature of academic environments. They recruited students, researchers, and faculty members, sometimes using coercion or financial incentives, to steal valuable research and technological innovations.

In the corporate world, China employed a tactic known as "economic espionage." Chinese spies infiltrated American businesses, particularly those involved in critical sectors like technology, pharmaceuticals, and manufacturing. They stole proprietary information and used it to replicate American products, undermining U.S. companies and boosting China's economic power.

Moreover, China leveraged its extensive diaspora community, often pressuring Chinese Americans to act as informants or agents. This tactic sowed distrust and fear within the community, further complicating efforts to identify and counter Chinese espionage activities.

One high-profile case involved "Agent Zhang," a Chinese national who had worked his way into a prominent Silicon Valley tech company. Over the years, he had managed to exfiltrate terabytes of data, including cutting-edge AI research and cybersecurity protocols, severely compromising American technological leadership.

The North Korean Saboteurs

Though smaller in scale, North Korea's espionage efforts were no less dangerous. The Reconnaissance General Bureau (RGB), North Korea's primary intelligence agency, focused on cyber warfare and sabotage.

North Korean hackers, operating from within their isolated homeland, launched a series of devastating cyberattacks on American infrastructure. These attacks targeted everything from financial institutions to power grids, aiming to create chaos and destabilize the nation.

Additionally, North Korean operatives engaged in smuggling and illicit trade, using American soil as a base for their criminal enterprises. The profits from these activities funded Pyongyang's nuclear and missile programs, posing a direct threat to global security.

One particularly notorious operative, "Mr. Kim," had established a network of front companies in the United States. Through these entities, he laundered money, procured restricted technologies, and facilitated contraband smuggling. His operations funded North Korea's clandestine projects and evaded international sanctions.

Unmasking the Shadows

The Counterintelligence Effort

As the scale of foreign espionage became apparent, American intelligence agencies launched a comprehensive counterintelligence effort. The FBI, CIA, and NSA worked tirelessly to identify and neutralize spies in the United States.

Advanced surveillance techniques, cyber forensics, and human intelligence (HUMINT) were deployed to track and apprehend foreign operatives. The process was painstakingly slow and fraught with challenges, as spies were adept at covering their tracks and blending into the fabric of American society.

Public awareness campaigns were initiated to educate citizens and corporations about the threat of espionage. Vigilance and cooperation from the private sector became crucial in detecting and thwarting foreign intelligence activities.

High-Profile Cases and Arrests

Several high-profile arrests highlighted the success of the counterintelligence campaign. Vladimir, the Russian spy embedded in the defense contractor, was apprehended in a dramatic raid. His capture led to the unraveling of a more extensive network of Russian operatives, providing valuable intelligence on Moscow's espionage strategies.

Agent Zhang's arrest sent shockwaves through Silicon Valley, prompting tech companies to reevaluate their security protocols and implement stricter measures to protect sensitive information. The case underscored the importance of vigilance in the face of sophisticated foreign threats.

Mr. Kim's network was dismantled through a coordinated operation involving multiple federal agencies. The crackdown on his illicit activities disrupted North Korean smuggling routes and significantly affected Pyongyang's financial channels.

The Resilience of Democracy

The unmasking of these foreign spies was a testament to the resilience of American democracy. Despite the sophisticated efforts to undermine it, the United States demonstrated its capacity to defend itself against overt and covert threats.

The lessons learned from these espionage cases strengthened national security measures and fostered a more vigilant and united society. The collaboration between government agencies, private enterprises, and ordinary citizens became a cornerstone of the nation's defense against future espionage activities.

Implications for U.S. National Security

Vulnerability Exploitation

Russia's actions could embolden other adversaries, such as China and North Korea, to exploit perceived vulnerabilities. Coordinated military posturing by these nations could lead to multiple, geographically dispersed threats, complicating U.S. strategic planning and response.

Russian Invasion

Alaska: Russian forces, having amassed near the border, would launch a surprise invasion into Alaska. Their objectives would be to capture key oil fields and strategic military bases, including Eielson Air Force Base and Fort Wainwright. The harsh terrain and climate would make a prolonged defense difficult for U.S. forces that are already spread thin.

In Kotzebue, Alaska's small, quiet town, the residents lived in harmony with the harsh but beautiful Arctic environment. The long winter nights and the cold, crisp air were constants. On a particularly frigid evening, as the aurora borealis painted the sky with its ethereal glow, the townspeople noticed an unusual sight on the horizon—distant, moving lights that flickered and swayed like a serpent of fire.

As dawn broke, the true nature of the spectacle became clear. A massive Russian army, clad in winter camouflage, advanced steadily through the snow-laden terrain. Tanks, armored personnel carriers, and infantry columns stretched as far as the eye could see. The ground trembled under the weight of their advance, and the air buzzed with the hum of engines and tracks clatter.

Chapter 3: The Call to Arms

Word of the invasion spread like wildfire. Governor Lisa Harding convened an emergency session with military leaders and local officials in

Anchorage. The gravity of the situation was undeniable. Russian forces were advancing southward with an apparent intent to seize critical infrastructure and the army bases.

Colonel Jack Reynolds, stationed at Joint Base Elmendorf-Richardson, was tasked with organizing the defense. His firm and resolute voice echoed through the halls as he addressed his troops: "We are the first line of defense. We hold the line here for our homes, families, and country."

The Alaskan National Guard, local militias, and volunteers mobilized quickly. In Fairbanks, residents fortified their homes and gathered supplies, preparing for a siege. Drawing on their ancestral knowledge of the land, the indigenous communities joined forces with the defenders, using their expertise to navigate and survive the harsh conditions.

The March of the Red Giants

The Russian advance was relentless. Led by General Viktor Sokolov, a seasoned strategist, the invasion force moved with precision and coordination. Their objective was clear: capture Anchorage and establish a foothold in North America. The element of surprise and his forces' initial successes bolstered Sokolov's confidence.

As the Russian army marched through the rugged terrain, they encountered resistance from small bands of Alaskan defenders. Though seemingly insignificant, these skirmishes slowed their progress and inflicted unexpected casualties. The defenders employed hit-and-run tactics, ambushing supply convoys and disrupting communication lines.

In the village of Noatak, a group of local hunters and trappers led by Elias Kavik staged a daring raid on a Russian patrol. Using their intimate knowledge of the land, they ambushed the patrol at a narrow pass, using the natural terrain to their advantage. The surprise attack resulted in a resounding victory, boosting the morale of the Alaskan defenders.

Beneath the Ice

Russian submarines moved with stealth and precision beneath the icy waters of the Bering Sea. These silent hunters, equipped with advanced stealth technology and armed with an array of missiles and torpedoes, played a crucial role in supporting the invasion of Alaska. Their mission was to disrupt American naval operations, gather intelligence, and support the advancing Russian ground forces.

The Submarine Fleet

Russia's Northern Fleet, a formidable force that included nuclear-powered submarines like the Borei-class and Yasen-class, had been mobilized for Operation "Northern Blizzard." These submarines were among the most advanced in the world, capable of launching ballistic missiles and conducting covert operations deep within enemy waters.

Admiral Sergei Morozov, a seasoned naval commander, oversaw the submarine operations. His orders were clear: maintain a blockade, disrupt U.S. supply lines, and gather intelligence on American naval movements.

The submarines coordinated closely with surface ships and air units, forming a triad of power that aimed to control the maritime domain.

Disrupting American Naval Operations

As the invasion began, Russian submarines positioned themselves strategically along the expected routes of American naval reinforcements. Their primary targets were the U.S. Navy's supply and logistics vessels, crucial for maintaining the flow of troops and equipment to the Alaskan front.

The submarines executed their mission in the ocean's dark depths with lethal efficiency. One such vessel, the Yasen-class submarine Severodvinsk, identified a convoy of American supply ships heading toward Anchorage. Moving silently through the water, Severodvinsk closed in on its prey. With a sudden burst of activity, it launched a volley of torpedoes, striking multiple targets and causing chaos in the convoy.

The explosions echoed through the cold waters, and within minutes, several American ships were crippled, their supplies lost to the sea. The attack forced the remaining ships to scatter, delaying the delivery of crucial reinforcements and supplies to the defenders in Alaska.

Intelligence and Electronic Warfare

Russian submarines also played a vital role in intelligence gathering and electronic warfare. Equipped with advanced sensors and surveillance equipment, they monitored U.S. naval movements and communication networks. Submarines like the Borei-class Alexander Nevsky collected valuable data on American patrol routes, fleet compositions, and defense strategies.

This intelligence was relayed back to Russian command, allowing them to adjust their strategies and stay one step ahead of the U.S. forces. Additionally, the submarines engaged in electronic warfare, jamming American communications and radar systems, further complicating the coordination of U.S. naval operations.

Supporting the Ground Invasion

Beyond their disruptive and intelligence-gathering roles, Russian submarines provided direct support to the ground invasion. They launched cruise missiles targeting American coastal defenses and military installations. These precision strikes created openings for the advancing Russian forces, softening resistance and sowing confusion among the defenders.

One notable attack was carried out by the Borei-class submarine Vladimir Monomakh. Positioned off the coast near Nome, it launched a series of Kalibr cruise missiles at vital military facilities, including radar stations and supply depots. The strikes were devastatingly compelling, knocking out critical infrastructure and paving the way for Russian ground forces to advance with less resistance.

America's Response

President Perrin's Decision: With the Russian threat emerging in the north, President Perrin is forced to make a tough decision. Realizing that the U.S. military is spread too thin across the globe, she recalls American troops from overseas, redirecting them to defend the homeland. The troops are divided between Alaska and California, with the most immediate threats receiving most of the forces.

The Siege of Anchorage

As the Russian forces approached Anchorage, the city became a fortress. Barricades were erected, and defensive positions fortified. The citizens, from shopkeepers to schoolteachers, joined the effort, determined to protect their homes. The spirit of resilience and unity permeated the air.

The first significant confrontation occurred on the outskirts of the city. Russian artillery pounded the defenses while waves of infantry and armored vehicles pushed forward. The defenders, though outnumbered, fought with unmatched ferocity. The battle raged for days, with both sides suffering heavy losses.

Amidst the chaos, Colonel Reynolds orchestrated a daring counterattack. Under the cover of darkness, a battalion of U.S. Marines and Army Rangers launched a flanking maneuver, targeting the Russian artillery positions. The surprise assault caught the invaders off guard, silencing their big guns and providing a much-needed respite for the defenders.

The Opposition

The Alaskan wilderness was a stark, lonely place, especially in the dead of winter. The cold air bit through the layers of clothing worn by the small band of soldiers who had managed to survive the first onslaught of the Russian invasion. The world they knew had been turned upside down. The war had escalated faster than anyone could have predicted, and the alliance between China and Russia had caught the United States off guard.

Sergeant Alex Brian peered through the scope of his rifle, scanning the treeline for any sign of movement. His breath formed small clouds of vapor in the frigid air. Beside him, Corporal Sarah Diaz adjusted her position, her fingers flexing nervously around the grip of her rifle.

"See anything?" she asked, her voice low but tense.

"Not yet," Brian replied. "But they're out there. I can feel it."

Behind them, the rest of their squad, a ragtag group of soldiers, huddled around a small, makeshift fire hidden deep in a snow-covered cave. Private Jake "Kruger" Thompson, the youngest of the group, was doing his best to warm his hands while Private First Class Mike "Bear" Kowalski kept an eye on their limited rations.

"How long do you think we can hold out here?"

Kruger asked, his voice shaking more from fear than the cold.

"Long as we need to," Bear grunted.

"No one's coming to save us, so we're alone."

The reality of their situation had settled in. Their base had been overrun two days earlier. Communications with the outside world were cut off, leaving them isolated behind enemy lines. The invasion had been swift, with Russian forces pouring into Alaska under the cover of darkness while Chinese troops had launched a coordinated strike on the West Coast.

The squad's mission now was simple: survive and disrupt the enemy as much as possible.

"Brian," a voice crackled over the radio, barely audible over the static.

Lieutenant Matthews was the only officer left alive from their original company. He had been separated from them during the chaos of the initial attack but had managed to stay in contact sporadically.

"Brian here, sir," he replied, keeping his voice low.

"There's a movement to the east of your position. Recon team spotted a Russian

patrol heading your way. It looks like they're sweeping the area."

They were running low on ammunition and supplies, and a firefight in these conditions could be suicide. But there was no choice—they had to hold their ground.

"Understood, sir. We'll be ready," Brian said.

Diaz nudged Brian and pointed towards the treeline. A glint of metal caught his eye, and sure enough, there was movement—slow, deliberate, and systematic. The Russians were approaching, using the dense forest as cover.

"Everyone, get ready," Brian whispered into his radio.

The squad moved with practiced efficiency, extinguishing the fire and taking up defensive positions around the cave entrance. The snow muffled their movements, but every crunch underfoot sounded deafening in the tense silence.

As the first Russian soldier broke through the treeline, Brian took a deep breath, steadying his aim. He could see the enemy soldier now, his face obscured by a balaclava, his eyes scanning the area for signs of life.

"Wait for it..." Brian muttered, his finger hovering over the trigger. He had to time this perfectly—one shot to remove the point man, and then his team would spring the ambush.

The Russian soldier paused, his head tilting slightly as if he had heard something. Brian's heart raced. Any second now...

An explosion rocked the forest, throwing snow and debris into the air. Brian's shot rang out a split second later, catching the Russian soldier in the chest. Chaos erupted as the rest of the squad opened fire, and their carefully laid ambush sprung.

The Russians were caught off guard but quickly regrouped, returning fire brutally. Brian ducked behind cover as bullets whizzed past him, thudding into the snow and rocks around him.

"Kruger, get the MG set up!" Brian shouted.

Kruger scrambled to position the squad's machine gun, setting it up behind a rocky outcrop. The heavy weapon roared to life, its steady stream of fire forcing the Russians to take cover.

But the enemy was relentless. More soldiers poured into the clearing, and Brian saw they were bringing up heavier weapons—grenade launchers and RPGs. The situation was rapidly spiralling out of control.

"We need to fall back!" Bear shouted over the din of battle.

Brian knew he was right. They couldn't hold this position much longer. But where could they go? The Russian forces were everywhere, and the unforgiving Alaskan wilderness offered little in the way of safe refuge.

"Matthews, we're getting overrun here!" Brian called into his radio. "We need

extraction, now!"

"Negative, Brian," Matthews replied, his voice grim. "No extraction available.

You're on your own. Make for the secondary rendezvous point. Good luck."

The line went dead, and Brian felt a cold knot of fear settle in his gut. They were truly alone now.

"Fall back!" Brian ordered. "Head for the ridge—move, move, move!"

The squad began to retreat, covering each other as they moved deeper into the forest. The Russians pursued them, their shouts growing louder and their footsteps crunching through the snow close behind.

Brian knew they were running out of time and options. They wouldn't last the night if they didn't find a way to shake their pursuers.

The Escape

The squad moved quickly through the forest, the deep snow hampering their progress. The ridge Brian had mentioned was a steep, rocky outcrop, partially obscured by trees and underbrush, offering some cover but little solace. The sound of gunfire and shouted orders echoed through the trees, pushing them onward.

Brian led the way, his mind racing as he tried to devise a plan. The ridge was their best chance to gain the high ground, but it was also a dead end—there would be no retreat once they were up there. He hoped their pursuers wouldn't risk following them into such rugged terrain.

Behind him, Bear was helping Kruger, who had taken a bullet grazing his leg. The young soldier was limping but kept pace, gritting his teeth against the pain.

"Almost there!" Brian called back, urging his team forward. The ridge loomed ahead, a dark silhouette against the pale sky.

They reached the base of the ridge just as the first of the Russian soldiers broke through the treeline behind them. Bullets whizzed past, splintering tree trunks and kicking up snow. Brian returned fire, covering Diaz as she scrambled up the rocky slope.

"Go, go, go!" Brian shouted, laying down suppressive fire.

The squad moved as one, ascending the ridge as fast as possible. The steep incline was treacherous; more than once, one slipped, but they kept going.

They were breathless and cold but alive when they reached the top. Brian dropped to one knee, quickly scanning the area below. The Russians were advancing but cautiously aware that they were at a disadvantage now.

"Set up a defensive perimeter," Brian ordered, his voice firm despite the adrenaline coursing through him.

"We make our stand here."

Diaz positioned herself behind a boulder, her rifle trained on the approach. Despite his injury, Kruger set up the machine gun again, and Bear checked their remaining ammunition.

"We don't have much left," Bear grumbled. "This isn't going to be pretty."

"We hold them off as long as possible," Brian replied. "We don't let them take this ridge."

The first Russian soldier appeared at the base of the ridge, cautiously advancing. Brian fired, taking him down with a single shot. The others opened, unleashing a barrage of bullets that forced the Russians to retreat temporarily.

But Brian knew it was only a matter of time before they regrouped and tried again.

As they caught their breath, a thought struck Brian. He reached for his map, quickly unfolding it. His eyes scanned the terrain, looking for anything to give them an edge.

"There," he muttered, pointing to a narrow pass that cut through the ridge further to the west. "We can use that to flank them. If we can get through there, we might be able to circle and hit them from behind."

"It's risky," Diaz said, her brow furrowed. "But it's better than waiting for them to wear us down."

"We leave now," Brian decided. "Kruger, can you move?"

Kruger nodded, his face pale but determined. "I can make it."

"Good. Diaz, take point. Bear, cover the rear. Let's move."

The squad began their trek along the ridge, keeping low to avoid detection. The pass was narrow and treacherous, but it provided cover for the advancing Russians. Brian's heart pounded in his chest as they made their way through. He knew they were gambling everything on this maneuver.

Finally, they emerged on the other side of the pass, coming out above the Russian position. The enemy soldiers were still focused on the ridge where they had last seen the Americans, unaware their prey had slipped behind them.

Brian signaled to his team, and they moved into position. This was their chance.

"On my mark," Brian whispered. "Three... two... one... Now!"

The squad opened fire, catching the Russians completely off guard. Brian's rifle cracked as he took down one enemy after another. Kruger's machine gun roared to life, mowing down the advancing soldiers. Bear tossed a grenade into a cluster of Russians, the explosion sending bodies flying.

The ambush was devastating. The Russians, disoriented and caught between two fronts, began to fall back in disarray. Brian's squad pressed the advantage, pushing the enemy down the ridge and into the forest below.

After several minutes of intense fighting, the gunfire began to die down. The remaining Russian soldiers were in full retreat, disappearing into the trees. Brian's squad stood victorious, their breaths coming in ragged gasps.

"We did it," Diaz said, lowering her rifle.

Brian nodded, but his mind was already racing ahead. This was just one skirmish in a much larger war. Although they had won this battle, the Russian and Chinese forces were still advancing across Alaska and the rest of North America. The road ahead was long and uncertain.

"We need to keep moving," Brian said, his voice steady. "There's a lot more work to do."

The squad gathered their gear and descended the ridge's other side, heading deeper into the Alaskan wilderness. The night was far from over, and they knew the real fight was only beginning.

As Brian's squad crested the ridge, they saw a sight that froze them in their tracks. Below, in the valley spread out before them, Russian tanks lined up in a formidable row, their hulking forms shrouded in mist and snow. The ground trembled slightly as the engines rumbled, and the unmistakable sound of tank treads grinding over frozen earth echoed in the cold morning air.

Brian's heart sank. This was it—the end of the line.

"Well, this it!" Bear muttered, his voice barely audible over the low growl of the tanks. "We're out of options, Sarge."

Brian couldn't argue. They were outnumbered, outgunned, and out of time. He glanced at his team—Diaz, her jaw set in grim determination; Kruger, leaning heavily on his rifle, still wounded but resolute; Bear, ever the warrior, even in the face of certain death; and Elena, the newest member of their ragtag group, who had found herself caught in a battle she never asked for.

"There's no way around them," Diaz said, her voice tight. "If we try to run, they'll mow us down before we make it ten yards."

Brian knew she was right. The valley was a kill zone and the tanks had it locked down. There was no cover, no escape. The realization settled over him like a heavyweight, but he refused to let despair take hold. They might not survive this, but they wouldn't go down without a fight.

"We can't let them take us alive," Kruger said, his voice shaky but firm. "We've got to hit them with everything we've got."

"Agreed," Brian said, his voice steady despite the fear gnawing at the edges of his mind. "We make our stand here. If we go out, we take as many of them as possible."

Bear grunted in approval. "Let's make it hurt."

The squad moved quickly, taking up positions along the ridge. They had precious little ammunition left, and even fewer grenades, but they prepared for the final assault with grim determination. There was no time for second thoughts, no room for hesitation.

Brian crouched behind a rocky outcrop, and his rifle trained on the lead tank. He knew their rifles would barely scratch the paint, but they had to try. Maybe, just maybe, they could disable one of the tanks and cause enough chaos to buy themselves a few more minutes.

The tanks began to move, slowly rolling forward like an unstoppable juggernaut. The ground trembled beneath them, the noise growing louder as they advanced. Brian took a deep breath, steadying his aim.

"On my mark," he said, his voice calm. "Three... two... one... Fire!"

The squad unleashed a desperate volley of fire, their bullets pinging uselessly off the thick armour of the tanks. Brian aimed for the tank's optics, hoping to blind the behemoth and slow it down, but the rounds bounced harmlessly off.

The tanks responded with terrifying efficiency. The lead tank's turret swivelled, its massive cannon lining up with their position. Brian's heart raced as he watched the barrel lower, knowing what was coming.

"Get down!" he shouted, diving for cover just as the cannon fired.

The explosion was deafening, a thunderous roar that shook the ridge. The blast threw Brian and the others to the ground, showering them with dirt and debris. The rock they had been using for cover was obliterated, exposing them.

Brian's ears rang as he scrambled to his feet, his vision blurred from the shockwave. He saw Diaz pulling Kruger to his feet, blood trickling down her face from a cut on her forehead. Bear was already on his feet, firing his last few rounds at the approaching tanks.

"Fall back!" Brian yelled, though he knew there was nowhere to fall back to. It was instinct—keep moving, keep fighting.

The squad retreated a few paces, but there was no escape. The tanks were closing in, and Brian could see the infantry following in their wake, Russian soldiers advancing with cold precision.

Brian's mind raced. He had one grenade left, a single explosive that wouldn't do much against a tank, but it was all they had. He pulled the pin, gripping it tightly as he prepared to make his final move.

"Diaz, Kruger, Bear... it's been an honor," Brian said, his voice filled with a quiet resolve. "Let's make this count."

Diaz nodded, her eyes fierce. "We go down fighting."

Kruger swallowed hard, his hands shaking. "See you on the other side."

Bear gave a grim smile, his eyes hard. "Let's show these bastards what we're made of."

As the tanks rumbled closer, Brian stood tall, the grenade clutched in his hand. He waited until the lead tank was almost upon them, its turret swiveling to deliver the final blow.

Then, with a primal roar, Brian threw the grenade with all his strength, aiming for the gap between the tank's treads. The grenade sailed through the air, a small, desperate missile in the face of overwhelming odds.

It landed perfectly, disappearing beneath the tank's massive frame. There was a split second of silence, a moment suspended in time, and the explosion tore through the air.

The tank shuddered as the blast rocked its underside, the explosion not enough to destroy it, but enough to cripple it. The tank lurched to a halt, smoke billowing from beneath it. For a brief, fleeting moment, Brian felt a surge of triumph.

But it was short-lived. The other tanks continued their advance, their cannons zooming toward the ridge. Brian knew this was it—the end.

He turned to his team, his heart heavy but his spirit unbroken. "We did our best," he said, his voice filled with quiet pride. "We gave them hell."

And then the tanks fired.

The explosions were blinding, a wall of fire and destruction that consumed the ridge, the snow, and everything in its path. Brian felt the heat, the shockwave, the pain—then nothing.

The ridge fell silent, the only sound the rumble of the tanks as they rolled on, leaving nothing but scorched earth and broken bodies in their wake.

But in that final stand, in the face of impossible odds, Brian and his squad had shown what it meant to be soldiers—to fight, resist, and never give up. Their sacrifice was a testament to their courage, defiance, and unbreakable spirit.

The tanks moved on, but the memory of that last stand would linger, a reminder that even in the darkest times, some will stand against the tide, no matter the cost.

Chinese Invasion

West Coast: Chinese forces, using a combination of amphibious assaults and paratrooper deployments, would target major West Coast cities. Key targets included:

- **Los Angeles:** To disrupt the entertainment industry and major shipping ports.
- **San Francisco:** To cripple the tech industry in Silicon Valley.
- **Seattle:** To target aerospace companies and further disrupt the tech sector.

Chinese naval and air superiority in the Pacific would be crucial for sustaining supply lines and reinforcements.

The Dragon Descends

The once-tranquil coast of California was about to become the focal point of a ferocious military campaign. The Chinese invasion, meticulously planned and executed, sought to seize control of the West Coast with a diverse and formidable force. The operation, codenamed "Dragon's Claw," was a symphony of military precision and overwhelming firepower.

The Prelude: A Storm Brews

The invasion began with a series of coordinated cyberattacks and missile strikes. The skies over California lit up with the glare of incoming missiles, targeting key military installations and communication networks. Power grids faltered, and major cities were plunged into chaos. This initial phase was designed to cripple the region's ability to mount an effective defense and sow confusion among the population.

The Chinese People's Liberation Army (PLA) Navy began approaching as the digital smoke cleared. Massive amphibious assault ships, brimming with soldiers and equipment, cut through the Pacific waters, heading towards the California coast. The armada included aircraft carriers, destroyers, and amphibious landing craft, all orchestrated for the coming assault.

The Beachhead Assault

At dawn, the first waves of the invasion force hit the beaches of Southern California. The sight was overwhelming: dozens of amphibious assault vehicles (AAVs) and tanks surged from the landing craft, engines roaring as they plowed through the surf. Chinese Marine Divisions led the charge, their primary goal to establish a secure beachhead and push inland.

In Los Angeles, the beaches became the scene of intense combat. American defenders, comprised of National Guard units and local law enforcement, scrambled to respond. Despite their valiant efforts, they were outmatched by the PLA's advanced technology and superior numbers. The Chinese Marines, equipped with high-caliber artillery and advanced combat gear, quickly secured vital positions along the coast.

Infiltration and Disruption

As the Chinese forces secured their initial beachheads, airborne and special operations units began their covert operations. The sky was filled with the roar of transport aircraft and the flutter of parachutes as airborne assault units descended behind enemy lines. Their mission was to sow chaos and weaken American resistance before the main force advanced.

Chinese special operations forces, known as "Jianbing Teams," infiltrated urban centres and critical infrastructure. In Los Angeles, they targeted power plants, communication hubs, and military installations.

Their stealthy operations created widespread confusion, disrupting American command and control.

One notable operation involved the capture of the Los Angeles Convention Center. Chinese commandos, armed with cutting-edge stealth technology, infiltrated the facility and seized control. This strategic move allowed the PLA to establish a forward operating base in the city's heart, further complicating American efforts to mount a cohesive defense.

The Armoured Push

With the beachheads secured and critical infrastructure disrupted, the Chinese Armoured Divisions moved into action. Their tanks and mechanized infantry rolled through the Central Valley, a region crucial for maintaining supply lines and controlling key transportation routes.

The Central Valley became an epic battleground. Armoured units, including main battle tanks (MBTs) and armoured personnel carriers (APCs), engaged in fierce combat with American forces. The PLA's firepower and mobility pushed them forward rapidly, capturing towns and securing vital infrastructure.

Mechanized infantry units supported the advance, clearing pockets of resistance and holding territory captured by the tanks. The American response was fierce, with local militias and National Guard units engaging in guerrilla tactics to slow the advance. Despite their determination, the overwhelming force of the Chinese invaders made it a gruelling fight.

The Battle of the Sierra Nevada

The Sierra Nevada Mountains became a critical battleground as American forces regrouped to mount a counteroffensive. The rugged terrain provided a natural advantage for American troops, who used guerrilla tactics and ambushes to their advantage.

The PLA faced significant challenges in the mountains. The terrain hindered their mechanized units and made supply lines difficult to maintain. The American forces, now reinforced with specialized mountain warfare units, launched a series of coordinated attacks. They used precision-guided munitions and drone surveillance to target Chinese positions and disrupt their operations.

The invasion of California had unleashed chaos along the West Coast, with significant cities under the control of the advancing Chinese forces. The streets of Los Angeles and San Francisco were battlegrounds, and the Central Valley became a critical theatre of operations. Amidst the turmoil, one elite unit stood as a beacon of hope: the Navy SEALs.

Amid the chaos, a special operations mission was being formulated. Intelligence reports indicated that a crucial Chinese command center was located in the heart of San Francisco's Golden Gate area. The facility was coordinating logistics and reinforcements for the PLA's advance. A team of Navy SEALs was dispatched on Operation Tide breaker to neutralize this threat and turn the tide of the invasion.

SEAL Team 6, one of the most renowned units in the U.S. Navy, was selected for this high-stakes mission. The team, led by Commander Jack Reynolds, included a diverse group of specialists: demolition experts, snipers, and communications technicians. Their objective was clear: infiltrate the heavily fortified command center, gather intelligence, and execute a decisive strike to cripple the Chinese operations.

Infiltration: The Golden Gate Bridge

Under the cover of darkness, the SEALs approached the Golden Gate area, a region now heavily fortified by the PLA. The iconic Golden Gate Bridge, once a symbol of American strength, had become a critical strategic point, with Chinese forces using it to move troops and equipment.

Phase 1: The SEALs were inserted by stealthy fast boats and submarines, undetected, slipping through the coastal defenses. They approached the area from the Pacific Ocean, using the rugged coastline as cover. The insertion was precise, with the team splitting into smaller units to avoid detection.

Phase 2: Reconnaissance The SEALs conducted a thorough survey of the command center, which was situated in a fortified building near the bridge. They used drones and night-vision equipment to map out the facility's defenses and identify key entry points. Elite PLA troops guarded the command center, and the perimeter was secured with advanced surveillance systems.

Phase 3: Sabotage and Assault The team executed a coordinated assault. The demolition experts placed charges to disable critical defensive structures and create entry points. As explosions rocked the facility, the SEALs breached the perimeter and moved swiftly through the building.

The SEAL snipers provided overwatch, eliminating enemy sentries and providing real-time intelligence on enemy movements. Inside the command center, the team encountered fierce resistance from Chinese soldiers who were well-equipped and highly trained.

The Battle Within the Command Center

Engagement The SEALs fought their way through the building, engaging in close-quarters combat with PLA forces. The fight was intense, with both sides using advanced weaponry and tactics. The Seals' superior training and teamwork gave them an edge, but the Chinese defenders were determined to hold their ground.

Critical Moments One of the essential moments of the battle occurred in the facility's control room, where Commander Reynolds and his team confronted a high-ranking Chinese officer. The officer was coordinating reinforcements and providing strategic guidance to the PLA forces. Neutralizing him was essential to disrupting the Chinese command structure.

The firefight in the control room was fierce, with both sides taking heavy casualties. The SEALs managed to overcome the defenders and capture the officer, gaining valuable intelligence about Chinese plans and troop movements.

Destruction of the Facility With their objectives achieved, the SEALs planted explosives throughout the command center, setting up charges to destroy critical infrastructure. As the team made their escape, the building was engulfed in a series of explosions, collapsing the command center and eliminating a major strategic asset for the PLA.

Extraction and Aftermath

Escape The SEALs exfiltrated using the same stealthy methods as their insertion. They regrouped on their extraction boats and submarines, successfully evading PLA patrols and returning to friendly territory. The operation was a tactical success, significantly damaging the Chinese invasion efforts.

The battle's turning point was a daring assault on a critical Chinese command post on a high-altitude ridge. By leveraging their knowledge of the terrain and superior tactics, American forces captured the position, causing significant disarray among the Chinese troops. The successful operation marked the beginning of a sustained counteroffensive.

The PLA began a strategic withdrawal as American forces pushed the Chinese back towards the coast. The retreat was organized, but the losses sustained and the logistical challenges made it clear that the invasion failed to achieve its primary objectives.

In the aftermath, California faced the monumental task of rebuilding. The cities, once symbols of American prosperity, lay in ruins. Reconstruction efforts began earnestly, focusing on repairing infrastructure, restoring utilities, and addressing the humanitarian crisis.

International aid flowed in, supporting the displaced population's reconstruction and humanitarian needs. The American government launched a massive recovery effort, with a renewed focus on strengthening defenses and ensuring that the country was better prepared for future threats.

The invasion had geopolitical implications. U.S.-China relations were severely strained, leading to a reassessment of global alliances and military strategies. The conflict underscored vulnerabilities in national definitions and cybersecurity, prompting reforms and increased investment in advanced technologies.

The international community watched closely as the two superpowers navigated the complex aftermath of the conflict. The invasion reshaped global alliances and set the stage for a new era of geopolitical dynamics.

The Dragon's Claw invasion was a testament to the complexity and scale of modern warfare. The operation involved various military units, each crucial in executing a sophisticated and ambitious campaign. The resilience of the American forces and the spirit of the civilian resistance ultimately could not stop the endless wave of Chinese expanding their reach.

In the aftermath of Operation Tide Breaker, the world was abuzz with the news of SEAL Team 6's heroic mission. Their success in crippling a crucial Chinese command center was a significant blow to the invasion forces. But the victory came at a cost, as the Chinese military, enraged and determined, vowed to take revenge. What followed was a relentless pursuit to eliminate the elite SEALs who had dealt such a heavy blow to their operations.

The Pursuit Begins

Chinese Retaliation Following the destruction of the command center, the Chinese high command launched a covert operation to hunt down and eliminate SEAL Team 6. They quickly determined the elite unit's likely escape routes and potential hideouts. Using their advanced surveillance and intelligence networks, they tracked the SEALs' movements and began closing in.

Strategic Ambush Chinese intelligence operatives pinpointed the location of SEAL Team 6's temporary base of operations in the rugged terrain of Northern California. They then set in motion a plan to launch a coordinated assault aimed at eliminating the SEALs before they could regroup and launch further attacks.

The Ambush

Nightfall, under cover of night, the Chinese forces executed their plan. A combination of elite PLA special forces and highly trained reconnaissance units surrounded the SEALs' base. The terrain, shrouded in darkness and dense forest, provided the perfect setting for an ambush.

Infiltration Chinese operatives, using advanced stealth technology and suppressors, infiltrated the perimeter of the SEALs' camp. They planted listening devices and set up traps to neutralize the elite unit's defenses. The operatives were highly skilled in psychological warfare, aiming to strike at the heart of the SEALs' confidence.

Initial Assault As the SEALs settled in for the night, they were caught off guard by the explosion of the camp's outer defenses. The Chinese forces launched a multi-pronged attack, using a combination of small arms fire, grenades, and sophisticated electronic warfare tools to disrupt communications and navigation systems.

The Battle

Brave Resistance Despite the surprise attack, SEAL Team 6 responded with characteristic bravery and skill. The team fought fiercely, utilizing their training and expertise to counter the assault. They engaged the Chinese forces in intense close-quarters combat, demonstrating their superior tactics and firepower.

Critical Moment Amid the chaos, a crucial moment unfolded. A Chinese special forces team equipped with advanced thermal vision and silent weapons targeted the SEALs' command structure. They managed to infiltrate the inner defenses and engage Commander Jack Reynolds directly.

The confrontation was brutal. A seasoned leader, Reynolds fought bravely, but the Chinese operatives' precision and tactical advantage proved overwhelming. The attack was swift and lethal, resulting in the fall of Reynolds and several other key team members.

Trapped and Outnumbered As the battle raged, the SEALs became increasingly surrounded and outnumbered. Chinese reinforcements arrived, turning the tide decisively in their favor. Once robust, the SEALs' perimeter defenses were overwhelmed by the relentless assault. The combination of electronic warfare and physical attacks created a nearly insurmountable challenge.

The Fall of SEAL Team 6

Final Stand With their command structure compromised and their position increasingly untenable, the remaining members of SEAL Team 6 made a final stand. They fought with unparalleled bravery, determined to hold their ground and protect their comrades.

The Last Moments As dawn broke, the remnants of SEAL Team 6 were forced into a last-ditch defense. Having breached the camp and overwhelmed the defenses, the Chinese forces closed in. The final moments were a fierce and desperate struggle, with the SEALs fighting to the end.

Despite their extraordinary efforts, SEAL Team 6 was ultimately defeated. The surviving members were either killed in combat or captured. The loss of the elite unit was a devastating blow to American forces and a significant victory for the PLA.

Aftermath

Impact on the War The elimination of SEAL Team 6 was a significant propaganda victory for the Chinese military. It demonstrated their capability to strike at the heart of American special operations and struck a blow to the morale of U.S. forces. The loss also highlighted the challenges of modern warfare, where even the most elite units can fall prey to coordinated and determined adversaries.

Strategic Repercussions: In response to the loss, the U.S. military reassessed its strategies and increased efforts to counter Chinese advancements. The defeat underscored the need for improved intelligence, counter-surveillance, and resilience in the face of sophisticated enemy tactics.

Legacy of Bravery: The story of SEAL Team 6's final battle became a symbol of courage and sacrifice. Their heroism was honored, and their legacy inspired renewed determination among American forces and allies. Their sacrifice served as a poignant reminder of the cost of war, but more importantly, it underscored the enduring spirit of those who fought to protect freedom and security. This spirit can never be extinguished.

The Last Stand of SEAL Team 6

The sun dipped below the horizon, casting long shadows across the rugged terrain of Northern California. The dense forest, once a sanctuary for SEAL Team 6, now harbored a looming threat. The elite unit had been instrumental in the recent Operation Tide breaker, a mission severely disrupting Chinese military operations. Now, their enemies were closing in, determined to exact revenge.

The Ambush

Twilight Terror: The night was eerily quiet, broken only by the sounds of the forest and the occasional crackle of a campfire. The SEALs, known for their vigilance, were lulled into a false sense of security. The Chinese forces had surrounded their temporary base, using advanced stealth technology and surveillance to avoid detection.

Suddenly, the tranquillity was shattered by a series of explosions. Chinese special forces, equipped with state-of-the-art stealth gear, breached the perimeter with calculated precision. The night sky was illuminated by bursts of gunfire and the flares of grenades. Once a bastion of American strength, the camp was thrown into chaos.

Initial Assault: The Chinese forces, comprising elite PLA operatives and heavily armed reinforcements, launched a coordinated attack. The SEALs, with their renowned skill and resilience, quickly adapted. They scrambled to their positions, weapons ready, engaging the attackers with disciplined, controlled bursts of fire. The firefight was fierce, but the Seals' skill and resilience reassured all that they were in capable hands.

The Battle Unfolds

Inside the Camp, Amid the chaos, SEAL Commander Jack Reynolds orchestrated the defense with calm efficiency. His voice crackled over the radio, issuing commands and coordinating the team's efforts. The SEALs fought valiantly, holding their ground against the relentless assault. With their unyielding determination, the Chinese forces launched wave after wave of attacks, intensifying the battle's danger and stakes.

The attack was not just a frontal assault. Chinese operatives had infiltrated the camp, using the cover of night to place listening devices and set traps. The Seals' perimeter defenses were compromised, and the attackers began to close in on the camp's core.

Critical Moments: A crucial moment came when the Chinese forces breached the inner sanctum of the camp. A group of PLA special forces, equipped with advanced thermal vision and silent weapons, moved stealthily through the camp's center. Their objective was clear: neutralize the Seals' command structure.

Commander Reynolds and his team fought bravely as the enemy closed in. They engaged in close-quarters combat, their tactical expertise on full display. Reynolds personally confronted a high-ranking Chinese officer, their battle a brutal exchange of blows and gunfire. Despite Reynolds' exceptional skill and leadership, the Chinese officer's precision and the support of his elite team proved overwhelming.

Desperate Resistance

The Last Stand: As dawn approached, the SEALs became increasingly isolated and outnumbered. Chinese reinforcements continued to pour in, and the camp's defenses were slowly being overwhelmed. Now fighting for their survival and comrades' safety, the SEALs made a final, desperate stand.

The battle was intense and tragic. The SEALs fought with unwavering courage; their movements were a testament to their training and dedication. They utilized every resource, from heavy weaponry to improvised defenses. The sound of gunfire, explosions, and the screams of battle filled the air as the elite unit faced the onslaught.

Final Moments: In the final moments of the battle, the Seals' remaining forces were engaged in a fierce and desperate defense. Once a stronghold, they were a battleground of shattered equipment and fallen comrades. The Chinese troops, having breached the camp and neutralized most of the SEALs, closed in on the remaining defenders.

Commander Reynolds and the last of his team fought to the end, their bravery unwavering. Despite their superior numbers and equipment, the Chinese forces faced fierce resistance. The final stand was a testament to the Seals' unyielding spirit, their determination shining through despite the odds overwhelmingly against them.

The Aftermath

The Loss: As the sun rose, casting light on the battlefield, the camp lay in ruins. The bodies of SEAL Team 6 were scattered across the once-pristine forest, their sacrifice a stark reminder of the brutal cost of war. The Chinese forces, having achieved their objective, secured the area and began the grim task of documenting their victory.

Impact on the War: The loss of SEAL Team 6 was a significant blow to American forces. Their defeat, while tragic, highlighted the harsh realities of modern warfare and the relentless nature of their adversaries. The bravery and sacrifice of the SEALs were honored, and their story became a symbol of courage in the face of overwhelming odds.

Legacy: SEAL Team 6's legacy lives on, inspiring American forces and allies alike. Their final battle was remembered not only for its intensity but also for the extraordinary bravery displayed by each member of the team. The sacrifice of SEAL Team 6 became a rallying point for renewed determination and resilience in the fight for freedom and security.

The Battle in the Sierra Nevada

Initial Skirmishes: The first encounters between the Chinese forces and the Native American warriors were minor skirmishes. The tribes, familiar with the terrain, used guerrilla tactics to harass and disrupt the Chinese supply lines. Ambushes were frequent, with warriors striking quickly and then melting back into the dense forests. The Chinese soldiers, despite their superior technology and numbers, struggled to adapt to the hit-and-run tactics employed by the Native Americans.

A Clash of Cultures: The resistance forces, trained in modern warfare, were initially caught off guard by the fierce resistance they encountered. The Native American warriors, armed with a mix of traditional weapons like bows and tomahawks and modern firearms, fought with tenacity and determination that surprised their enemies.

The tribes utilized the terrain to their advantage. The Sierra Nevada's dense forests, cliffs, and hidden valleys provided perfect cover for ambushes and surprise attacks. The warriors moved silently through the mountains, striking at vulnerable points in the Chinese advance. The Chinese soldiers, burdened by heavy equipment and unfamiliar with the land, were disadvantaged.

The Spirit of Resistance: As the battle intensified, the Native American warriors drew strength from their deep connection to the land. The Sierra Nevada was not just a battlefield but their home, a place of spiritual significance. This connection fuelled their resolve, turning each skirmish into a fight for survival and sovereignty.

The tribes employed traditional war cries, drums, and chants, which echoed through the mountains, creating an eerie atmosphere that unnerved the Chinese soldiers. These tactics had a profound psychological impact, causing confusion and fear among the invading forces.

The Turning Point

The Battle of Echo Pass: The Chinese commanders, realizing that they needed to break the Native American resistance, concentrated their forces on a strategic location known as Echo Pass. This narrow pass was a critical chokepoint that, if secured, would allow the Chinese to control access to the entire region.

The Native American warriors, aware of Echo Pass's importance, prepared for a decisive battle. They fortified the pass, setting up traps and using the natural terrain to create defensive positions. The ensuing battle was fierce, with both sides fully committed to victory.

Fierce Combat: The Chinese forces launched a full-scale assault on Echo Pass, deploying infantry, armored vehicles, and air support. The Native American warriors, though outnumbered and outgunned, fought with unmatched bravery. The battle raged for hours, with the pass becoming a deadly gauntlet of fire and steel.

The Chinese soldiers were bogged down in the narrow pass despite their technological and firepower advantages. The Native Americans, fighting with a combination of ancient tactics and modern guerrilla warfare, inflicted heavy casualties on the invaders. The warriors' knowledge of the land and determination to protect it turned the tide in their favour.

The Arrival of Gray Wolf

As the flames of resistance spread across California, warriors from distant lands began to heed the call to arms. Among them was a warrior from the vast plains of Wyoming known as **Gray Wolf**. His journey from the windswept mountains of his homeland to the rugged Sierra Nevada would become a tale of determination, unity, and the unbreakable bond between warriors fighting for their people.

The Journey of Gray Wolf

The Call from the West Gray Wolf was a warrior of the Northern Arapaho tribe who had lived on the high plains of Wyoming for generations. A respected hunter and tracker, he was known for his sharp instincts and unwavering resolve. When news of the Chinese invasion reached the Northern Arapaho, Gray Wolf felt the pull of destiny. He knew that his skills and strength were needed and that the fight in California was not just for land but for the survival of their way of life.

Gray Wolf's Conversion

One evening, as the sun dipped behind the mountains, casting long shadows over the camp, Gray Wolf approached Brother Michael, a minister in the church of Christ, with a question that weighed on his heart.

"Brother," Gray Wolf began, his voice thoughtful and steady, *"what do your people believe happens when a man dies?"*

Brother Michael looked at Gray Wolf with compassion, sensing the gravity of his question. *"We believe that when a man dies, his soul returns to God, who gave it,"* he replied. *"If he has followed Christ and lived according to God's commandments, he will be welcomed into heaven, a place of eternal peace and rest."*

Gray Wolf listened intently, nodding as he absorbed the words. *"And what of a warrior, one who has taken many lives?"* he asked, his voice tinged with the weight of his experiences.

Brother Michael placed a reassuring hand on Gray Wolf's shoulder. *"The Lord is merciful,"* he said. *"If a man's heart is pure, and he has fought to protect the innocent and uphold justice, there is forgiveness in Christ. No sin is too great to be washed away if a man truly seeks redemption."* At that moment, Gray Wolf confessed to Jesus, was taken to the river, and baptized.

These words stayed with Gray Wolf in the days that followed. He found himself praying quietly in his way, seeking the Creator's guidance and the peace promised by the Christian God.

Off to War

He left his family and travelled west, where the battle raged. His journey took him through the Rocky Mountains and the Great Basin, a trek that tested his endurance and spirit. But Gray Wolf was determined; the stories of the resistance in the Sierra Nevada fuelled his resolve.

Joining the Fight: When Gray Wolf arrived in California, he sought out the leaders of the resistance. Word of his arrival spread quickly, and he was welcomed by Red Hawk and the warriors of the Eagle's Claw. Though they came from different lands, they shared a common purpose and a deep respect for each other's traditions.

Gray Wolf's arrival brought a new energy to the camp. He shared his knowledge of tracking and hunting, skills that would prove invaluable in the guerrilla warfare tactics employed by the resistance. His quiet strength and deep connection to the land quickly earned him the respect of the other warriors.

The Battle of Red Peak

A New Threat With the victory at Thunder Valley still fresh in their minds, the Chinese forces were determined to reclaim their lost ground. Their next target was **Red Peak**, a strategic location offering a commanding view of the surrounding area. The Chinese knew that if they could secure Red Peak, they could control the movement of resistance forces in the region.

Now bolstered by Gray Wolf's arrival, Red Hawk and the Eagle's Claw prepared for the inevitable assault. They knew that the battle for Red Peak would be one of the most challenging yet and that the outcome could shift the balance of the entire campaign.

Gray Wolf's Contribution As the warriors prepared for battle, Gray Wolf took on a crucial role. His experience as a tracker allowed him to anticipate the movements of the Chinese forces. He scouted the area around Red Peak, identifying potential ambush points and weaknesses in the enemy's approach.

Though different from the Sierra Nevada, his knowledge of the land translated well to the rugged terrain. Gray Wolf set traps along the paths he predicted the Chinese would take, using his skills to turn the environment into a weapon. He also trained the younger warriors in stealth, teaching them to move silently and strike without warning.

The Battle Unfolds At dawn, the Chinese forces launched their attack. The approach to Red Peak was steep and treacherous, and the invaders were forced to advance slowly, their heavy equipment struggling against the rough terrain. As they climbed, they encountered the traps Gray Wolf and his followers set tripwires that triggered rockslides, pits covered with branches, and concealed spikes.

The Eagle's Claw, with Gray Wolf among them, waited in the shadows. The warriors launched their ambush as the Chinese forces pushed further up the peak. Arrows rained from above, and the warriors struck with the speed and precision of a hawk diving on its prey.

Gray Wolf fought alongside Red Hawk, his tomahawk and bow cutting through the ranks of the Chinese soldiers. His movements were fluid and deliberate; every strike aimed to cripple and disorient the enemy. The battle was fierce, with the Chinese forces struggling to gain ground against the relentless attacks of the resistance.

A Moment of Unity: At a critical moment in the battle, the Chinese forces breached the defensive line. They poured into the heart of Red Peak, threatening to overrun the position. Red Hawk and Gray Wolf fought side by side, their backs against a rocky outcrop as they faced the advancing enemy.

In that moment, the bond between the two warriors—one from the Sierra Nevada, the other from the plains of Wyoming—was solidified. They fought as one, their movements in perfect harmony, a testament to the unity that had grown among the resistance. Their combined strength turned the tide, and the warriors of the Eagle's Claw rallied around them.

Victory and Brotherhood: As the sun began to set, the Chinese forces, battered and demoralized, were forced to retreat. The Battle of Red Peak had been won, thanks in no small part to Gray Wolf's contributions. The victory was significant for the ground it secured and the spirit of unity it embodied.

After the battle, Red Hawk and Gray Wolf stood atop Red Peak, looking over the land they had fought to protect. Their respect was palpable, and their bond was now one of brotherhood. Gray Wolf's journey from Wyoming had brought him to the heart of a battle that would shape the future of the resistance, and his presence had made a difference.

Grey Wolf's Last Stand

Though outnumbered and outgunned, the resistance fighters were not ready to surrender. Having fought in countless battles since his arrival from Wyoming, Gray Wolf knew that the time had come for a final, decisive stand. The battle would take place at **Iron Ridge**, a narrow pass that was the last barrier between the Chinese army and the heart of the resistance.

Gray Wolf and his Braves, now fewer in number but hardened by the long campaign, prepared for what they knew would be their final battle. The air was tense, and the mountains were silent as if holding their breath. Gray Wolf gathered his warriors one last time, speaking to them in the Arapaho language that had guided them through every challenge.

A Leader's Last Words

"Nii'ookoo," Gray Wolf began his voice steady but carrying the moment's weight. *("My brothers, we have come to the end of our journey.")* He looked into the eyes of each of his Braves, seeing in them the same resolve that had carried them through so many battles.

"Hinono'eitiit neetnii3itoo'uu, niiho'oowoo," he continued, his voice filled with quiet pride. *("Our ancestors have walked with us, and we have fought with honor.")*

One of the Braves, his face marked by the scars of war, stepped forward. *"Nii'eihii3ei,"* he said, his voice trembling with emotion. *("Gray Wolf, you have led us with courage and wisdom. We will follow you to the end.")*

Gray Wolf placed a hand on the warrior's shoulder, nodding solemnly. *"Nii'iiteiht bii'coo'uni,"* he said, his voice softening. *("Today, we fight not for victory, but for the honor of our people.")*

He turned to face Iron Ridge, the narrow pass that would be their battleground. The Chinese forces were already moving into position, their numbers overwhelming. Gray Wolf knew there was no hope of survival, but he was determined to make the enemy pay dearly for every inch of ground.

The Final Battle

The Chinese attack began with the thunder of artillery and shells exploding against the rocky slopes of Iron Ridge. Gray Wolf and his Braves took cover, waiting for the enemy to advance. When the first wave of soldiers moved into the pass, Gray Wolf gave the signal, and the Braves unleashed a torrent of arrows and bullets, catching the Chinese forces in a deadly crossfire.

The narrowness of the pass worked to the defenders' advantage, forcing the Chinese soldiers into a bottleneck where they became easy targets. But the enemy kept coming, wave after wave, their sheer numbers threatening to overwhelm the defenders.

Gray Wolf fought with the ferocity of a cornered wolf, his tomahawk and bow striking down enemies with deadly precision. Around him, his Braves fought with the same determination, knowing that this was their last stand. The battle was brutal and unforgiving, the pass becoming a graveyard of fallen warriors.

As the hours wore on, the resistance fighters began to fall, their numbers dwindling with each passing minute. Gray Wolf could see that the end was near but refused to retreat. He had made a promise to his people, and he would not abandon his post.

The Last Stand

In the final moments of the battle, the Chinese forces managed to break through the defensive line, pushing the remaining resistance fighters back to the highest point of Iron Ridge. Gray Wolf, now surrounded by the bodies of his fallen Braves, stood alone at the edge of the ridge.

With a fierce war cry, he charged into the midst of the enemy, his tomahawk flashing in the fading light. The Chinese soldiers, momentarily stunned by the sheer audacity of the attack, hesitated. But the numbers were too great, and Gray Wolf was soon surrounded.

Wounded and exhausted, Gray Wolf fought on, his every movement driven by the spirit of his ancestors. As the enemy closed in, he could feel the end approaching. But his heart had no fear—only a deep sense of peace.

"Niiho'oowoo," he whispered, raising his tomahawk one last time. *("For our people, for our land.")*

With a final, defiant cry, Gray Wolf struck down the nearest soldier, only to be overwhelmed by the others. The Chinese forces, recognizing the fierce resistance of the lone warrior, took a step back, giving him a moment of respect before the final blow.

As Gray Wolf fell to the ground, he looked up at the sky, the golden light of the setting sun casting a warm glow over the battlefield. With his last breath, he whispered a prayer to Jesus, the Savior he had chosen to follow.

"Jesus," Gray Wolf prayed, his voice faint but filled with conviction, *"be with me now as I enter paradise."*

Though he had been born and raised according to his people's traditions, Gray Wolf knew that following Jesus was a choice he made freely with his heart and soul. In that moment, he felt Christ's presence beside him, a comforting warmth that eased his pain and guided him toward the light.

As his spirit left his body, Gray Wolf felt a sense of peace unlike any he had ever known. He had fought with honour and would rest in the eternal paradise Jesus promised.

A Warrior's Rest

When the battle was over, Brother Michael and the surviving resistance fighters found Gray Wolf's body atop Iron Ridge. The minister knelt beside him, tears in his eyes as he offered a prayer for his soul.

"Lord Jesus," Brother Michael prayed, his voice filled with reverence, *"receive this warrior into Your kingdom. He chose to follow You, and now he rests in Your peace. Grant him the paradise You have promised."*

The resistance fighters gathered around, paying their respects to the man who had led them with courage and integrity. They buried Gray Wolf at the highest point of Iron Ridge, marking his grave with a simple cross—a symbol of the faith he had embraced in his final days.

Hawaii: North Korean forces, supported by Chinese naval units, would launch an assault on Hawaii. Their primary goal was to neutralize the U.S. Pacific Fleet stationed at Pearl Harbor and secure a forward base for further operations in the Pacific.

As tensions mounted, President Perrin remained resolute. She knew the road ahead would be fraught with challenges, but her determination to lead with integrity and strength never wavered. She convened her top advisors, ensuring every possible measure was taken to protect the nation and its interests.

In the face of an unprecedented threat, the world watched as a new chapter in history unfolded. Emily Perrin, the first woman President of the United States, stood at the helm of a nation poised to defend its ideals against formidable adversaries. The outcome of this geopolitical chess game would shape the future of international relations for years to come.

Those in power knew that America would falter; they didn't know how much of the country would be lost.

The Korean Assault on Hawaii

The Prelude to Invasion

Hawaii, the jewel of the Pacific, had long been considered a strategic stronghold for the United States. Its islands served as the gateway to the Pacific, a vital link in the American defenses stretching across the ocean. But in the chaotic tides of global war, Hawaii had become a coveted prize for those who sought to control the Pacific.

In the shadow of larger conflicts, North Korea, with the quiet backing of China, had been preparing for an audacious move: the invasion of Hawaii. For years, the North Korean military had been building its naval and air capabilities, using the cover of diplomatic engagement and economic negotiations to hide its true intentions. But the accurate plans were far more sinister.

The Silent Advance

The invasion began in the dead of night. North Korean submarines, equipped with advanced stealth technology, slipped through the Pacific, avoiding detection by American and Allied forces. These submarines carried elite units of North Korean commandos; seasoned veterans of the special operations forces who had been trained specifically for this mission.

Simultaneously, a fleet of North Korean warships, including destroyers and missile frigates, moved into position. These ships were armed with long-range missiles and advanced anti-aircraft systems, ready to challenge aerial or naval counterattacks. North Korea's new generation of fighter jets, designed with the help of Chinese engineers, were also on standby, prepared to strike at a moment's notice.

The initial assault targeted the communication and radar systems on the islands, with cyberattacks crippling Hawaii's defense networks. The U.S. military, caught off guard by the sudden onslaught, struggled to regain control of its systems as the North Korean forces closed in.

The First Strike

The first wave of the invasion struck Pearl Harbor, a name forever etched in American history. This time, the attack came not from the skies but from beneath the waves. North Korean submarines launched a barrage of torpedoes at the American naval vessels stationed there. Simultaneously, North Korean commandos, clad in black wetsuits and armed with silenced weapons, emerged from the water, infiltrating the naval base.

Their mission was clear: disable the American warships and take control of key installations before reinforcements could arrive. The commandos moved with precision, planting explosives and engaging in close-quarters combat with the surprised American forces. Despite fierce resistance, the North Koreans managed to inflict significant damage, sinking several ships and causing chaos within the base.

At the same time, North Korean missiles rained down on Hickam Air Force Base, targeting the runways and hangars to prevent any American aircraft from taking off. The attack was devastating, with several planes destroyed on the ground before they could even be scrambled. The airbase, one of the critical defense points in the Pacific, was left in disarray.

The Land Invasion

As the naval and air assault raged on, North Korean amphibious forces landed on the shores of Oahu. These troops were heavily armed and well-prepared for urban warfare. They moved quickly, capturing key positions and securing a foothold on the island. Although well-trained, the local Hawaiian defense forces were overwhelmed by the sheer scale and intensity of the assault.

The North Korean forces advanced toward Honolulu, the capital of Hawaii, with the intent of capturing the city and its vital infrastructure. The invaders met stiff resistance from American troops and local defense forces but pressed on, using their superior numbers and pre-planned tactics to their advantage.

The Battle for Honolulu

The battle for Honolulu was fierce and bloody. The city's streets became a battleground as American and Hawaiian forces fought to repel the invaders. The North Koreans, however, were relentless. They moved from building to building, engaging in brutal urban combat with the defenders. Civilians were caught in the crossfire, adding to the chaos and horror of the invasion.

Despite the overwhelming odds, the American and Hawaiian forces fought with determination. They knew that the fall of Honolulu would mean the loss of Hawaii, and they were not willing to let that happen. But the North Koreans were well-prepared, and their relentless assault began to take its toll.

The Conquest of Hawaii

The Korean Conquest of Hawaii

The Prelude to Domination

In the early stages of the Korean invasion, Hawaii had been a crucial target for North Korea's ambitious plans. Following their initial successful strikes on Oʻahu and Kauaʻi, the North Korean military, buoyed by their early victories, moved to consolidate their control over the Hawaiian Islands. With their grip tightening, Hawaii's fate hung in the balance.

The North Korean leadership, backed by Chinese support, meticulously planned the invasion. Their strategy was to seize control of the archipelago by overwhelming the islands with their military might and suppressing any resistance quickly. The goal was to establish a stronghold in the Pacific to serve as a strategic base for further operations and negotiations.

The Final Assault

With Oʻahu and Kauaʻi under partial control, the North Koreans turned their attention to the remaining islands: Molokaʻi, Lānaʻi, and Maui. The invasion strategy was clear—swift, decisive action to prevent the islands from rallying together and mounting a coordinated defense.

Molokaʻi and Lānaʻi: Quick Conquest

Rapid military operations characterized the invasion of Molokaʻi and Lānaʻi. North Korean forces landed on the beaches of Molokaʻi, encountering only minimal resistance. The local Hawaiian defense forces were ill-equipped and overwhelmed by the invaders' superior numbers and firepower. The North Koreans swiftly established control over the island's strategic points, setting up military installations and fortifications.

Similarly, Lāna'i fell quickly to the invading forces. The island's sparse population and lack of heavy defenses made it an easy target. The North Koreans utilized their naval superiority to block any attempts at resistance or evacuation, effectively cutting off Lāna'i from any potential support.

Maui: The Crucial Battle

With a larger population and more significant strategic importance, Maui became the focal point of the North Korean campaign. The island's rugged terrain and urban centres presented opportunities and challenges for the invaders.

The North Korean military executed a multi-pronged assault on Maui. Troops landed on the western coast near Lahaina and Kihei, while their naval forces blockaded the island's ports to prevent any escape or reinforcement. The initial landings were met with fierce resistance from residents and the remaining Hawaiian defense forces.

The battle for Maui was intense and protracted. The North Koreans employed a combination of overwhelming firepower, psychological warfare, and strategic encirclement. They used their advanced artillery and air support to bombard key positions and create chaos within the island's defenses. Urban centres like Wailuku and Kahului became battlegrounds, with the North Koreans pushing into the heart of the island.

The Fall of Maui

Despite their determination, the defenders of Maui faced insurmountable odds. The North Koreans' superior technology, coordination, and numbers began to turn the tide. As the North Korean forces pressed deeper into Maui, they systematically dismantled the island's defenses. They captured critical infrastructure, including power plants, communication hubs, and transportation networks.

One of the turning points in the battle was the capture of the island's main airport. With the airport under North Korean control, they could reinforce their troops and supply their operations more efficiently. The defenders, exhausted and outnumbered, struggled to mount a coherent defense.

As the North Korean forces tightened their grip on Maui, resistance began to crumble. Key defensive positions fell, and pockets of resistance were slowly eradicated. The final stages of the battle saw the North Koreans consolidating their control over the island, establishing their presence, and reinforcing their positions.

The Conquest of Hawaii

With Maui falling to the North Koreans, the entire Hawaiian archipelago was effectively under their control. The conquest of Hawaii marked a significant achievement for the North Korean regime. The islands, once a strategic stronghold of the United States, were now a symbol of their power and ambition.

The North Korean leadership imposed martial law across the islands. The local Hawaiian population faced harsh conditions under occupation, with strict curfews, limited freedoms, and severe reprisals against those who resisted. The invaders began an indoctrination campaign to solidify their control and eliminate any remaining opposition.

The Aftermath and Resistance

The fall of Hawaii was a devastating blow to the United States, but it also galvanized a new wave of resistance. Underground networks and guerilla groups formed after the invasion determined to resist the occupation and reclaim their homeland. These groups operated from hidden bases, conducting sabotage operations and raids against North Korean forces.

Internationally, the invasion drew condemnation and a renewed commitment to defending the Pacific. Recognizing Hawaii's strategic importance, the United States and its allies began planning their response. The struggle for Hawaii became a focal point in the broader conflict, symbolizing the challenges of the invasion and the resilience of those who fought to reclaim their land.

Legacy of the Invasion

The Korean conquest of Hawaii became pivotal in the more significant conflict. It demonstrated North Korea's strategic ambitions and the vulnerabilities of the American defense posture in the Pacific. The occupation left deep scars on the islands and their people but also inspired fierce resistance that would continue to shape the course of the war.

In the following years, the story of Hawaii's occupation and the resistance against it became a powerful symbol of courage and defiance. The invasion's legacy was a reminder of the high stakes of global conflict and the enduring strength of those who stand against oppression.

The North Korean leadership imposed martial law across the islands. The local Hawaiian population faced harsh conditions under occupation, with strict curfews, limited freedoms, and severe reprisals against those who resisted. The invaders began an indoctrination campaign to solidify their control and eliminate any remaining opposition.

The Aftermath and Resistance

The fall of Hawaii was a devastating blow to the United States, but it also galvanized a new wave of resistance. Underground networks and guerilla groups formed after the invasion determined to resist the occupation and reclaim their homeland. These groups operated from hidden bases, conducting sabotage operations and raids against North Korean forces.

Internationally, the invasion drew condemnation and a renewed commitment to defending the Pacific. Recognizing Hawaii's strategic importance, the United States and its allies began planning their response. The struggle for Hawaii became a focal point in the broader conflict, symbolizing the challenges of the invasion and the resilience of those who fought to reclaim their land.

The Korean conquest of Hawaii became pivotal in the more significant conflict. It demonstrated North Korea's strategic ambitions and the vulnerabilities of the American defense posture in the Pacific. The occupation left deep scars on the islands and their people but also inspired fierce resistance that would continue to shape the course of the war.

In the following years, the story of Hawaii's occupation and the resistance against it became a powerful symbol of courage and defiance. The invasion's legacy was a reminder of the high stakes of global conflict and the enduring strength of those who stand against oppression.

The Crisis in Alaska

As the global conflict intensified, Alaska was on the front lines of the struggle against invading forces. In advancing from the north, Russian troops had launched a major offensive into the Alaskan interior. Alaska's rugged terrain and harsh climate presented significant challenges, but the Russian military, equipped with heavy armour and air support, pressed on with their invasion.

The local Alaskan resistance, comprised of military personnel and civilian volunteers, fought bravely but was overwhelmed by the sheer scale of the invasion. The situation became dire as Russian forces closed in on key strategic positions and significant towns. The U.S. military recognized the situation's urgency and planned a daring rescue operation to support the beleaguered defenders.

The operation: Arctic Eagle

The operation, code-named **Arctic Eagle**, aimed to boost the Alaskan resistance by deploying elite units directly into the conflict zone. The mission involved a combined force of Army Rangers and Special Forces operators, specifically chosen for their expertise in high-risk, high-reward operations in extreme conditions.

Infiltration and Preparation

The Army Rangers, known for their exceptional airborne capabilities, were tasked with the initial insertion into the conflict zone. Their mission was to secure key landing zones and provide immediate support to the local defenders. The Special Forces operators, specializing in unconventional warfare and counterinsurgency, were assigned to surveillance, sabotage enemy operations, and support resistance efforts.

The plan called for a coordinated airborne assault. Under the cover of darkness, the Rangers and Special Forces would parachute into the Alaskan wilderness, avoiding Russian detection and making their way to the front lines.

The Para jump

The operation commenced on a freezing night with snowflakes swirling in the Arctic wind. The Rangers and Special Forces boarded their aircraft, their breath visible in the frigid air. As the planes approached the drop zones, the tension was palpable.

The first wave of Rangers leaped from the aircraft, their parachutes opening against the backdrop of the icy landscape. They descended into the snow-covered wilderness, landing near a strategically important town under siege. The Rangers quickly gathered their gear and began establishing defensive positions, preparing to repel enemy advances.

Following the Rangers, the Special Forces operators parachuted into their designated drop zones, carefully avoiding Russian radar and patrols. They aimed to blend in with the local resistance, gather intelligence, and launch coordinated strikes against Russian supply lines and command posts.

The Counterattack

With the Rangers securing the town and the Special Forces embedding with local resistance groups, the stage was set for a coordinated counteroffensive. Initially caught off guard by the sudden influx of elite troops, the Russian forces faced immediate challenges.

Skilled in urban and mountain warfare, the Rangers conducted a series of daring raids against Russian positions. Using their knowledge of the terrain, they executed ambushes and hit-and-run attacks, targeting critical Russian assets and disrupting their operations.

Simultaneously, the Special Forces operators provided crucial support to the resistance. They conducted reconnaissance missions to identify Russian vulnerabilities and coordinated with the local fighters to launch sabotage operations. Their expertise in guerrilla warfare and unconventional tactics proved invaluable in undermining the Russian advance.

The Russian forces faced mounting setbacks, so they were forced to reevaluate their strategy. The coordinated counteroffensive by the Rangers, Special Forces, and local defenders had significantly weakened their position, allowing the Alaskan resistance to regain ground.

The successful operation provided crucial support to the Alaskan defenders and demonstrated the effectiveness of joint operations and specialized tactics in complex environments. The bravery and skill of the

Rangers and Special Forces were hailed as a turning point in the defense of Alaska.

In the aftermath of Arctic Eagle, the region saw a resurgence of resistance and a renewed sense of hope. The efforts of the elite units, combined with the resilience of the local fighters, laid the groundwork for a sustained defense and eventual counteroffensive against the Russian invaders.

The Unexpected

In a coordinated operation that stunned U.S. intelligence, Chinese airborne divisions, equipped with cutting-edge technology and supported by precision airstrikes, have descended upon Alaska in waves. They landed behind American lines, effectively cutting off the SEALs and Rangers from their supply routes and reinforcements. The highly disciplined and well-trained paratroopers swiftly established control over key areas, setting up fortified positions that were nearly impregnable.

Caught between the advancing Russian forces and the newly entrenched Chinese paratroopers, the U.S. special operations units found themselves in an increasingly desperate situation. Their communications were disrupted, their supplies dwindled, and the harsh Arctic environment, once an ally, became a relentless adversary.

Isolated and outnumbered, the SEALs and Rangers continued to fight bravely, but their efforts were ultimately in vain. The combined might of the Russian and Chinese forces proved overwhelming. In a series of brutal engagements, the American units were systematically hunted down. The battles were fierce, but the outcome was never in doubt. Those who were captured faced a grim fate; they were interrogated, tortured, and eventually executed as a message to the remaining American forces.

By the end of the campaign, Alaska had fallen under the control, either dead or in captivity. The loss was a devastating blow to the United States, both strategically and psychologically. It marked a chilling escalation in the global conflict, a stark reminder of the growing alliance between two of the world's most potent adversaries.

The frozen wasteland of Alaska, once a symbol of American resilience and frontier spirit, had become the graveyard of its most elite warriors.

Planes Over Washington D.C.

The Invasion

A Coordinated Strike: The Russian invasion was meticulously planned. Satellite communications are disrupted, and cyberattacks cripple U.S. defense systems, creating confusion and hindering response efforts. In the early hours before dawn, Russian forces launch a surprise air assault, deploying thousands of paratroopers over Washington, D.C.

Paratrooper Deployment: The skies over Washington are filled with the sight of descending paratroopers, their chutes blending into the early morning fog. They land strategically across the city near the Capitol, the White House, and key military installations.

Swift Offensive: Russian forces move with precision and ruthless efficiency. Using advanced technology and well-trained special forces, they quickly overpower local National Guard units and security forces. Government buildings are targeted with surgical strikes, ensuring minimal resistance. Using EMP (Electromagnetic Pulse) weapons disables electronic devices, leaving Washington in disarray.

Fall of Washington

Capture of Key Government Figures: Within hours, Russian forces have secured the Capitol and the White House. Government officials, including the President, are taken hostage. The President, along with key cabinet members, is captured and held in an undisclosed location under heavy guard. The swift and brutal nature of the assault leaves the government in disarray, with no time to organize an adequate response.

Demolition of Symbolic Landmarks: To demoralize the American people, the invaders destroy iconic landmarks such as the Washington Monument and portions of the Capitol. Explosions rock the city, and smoke fills the air, a grim reminder of the fall of the nation's capital. The sight of these symbols of American power reduced to rubble sends shockwaves across the country.

Immediate Aftermath

Martial Law and Confusion: With Washington in ruins and the President captured, martial law is declared in many states. The chain of command is broken, and various military and political leaders across the country struggle to maintain order. Communication is sporadic, and panic spreads among the population.

The South Shall Rise Again

In the blistering heat of a Mississippi summer, a dense fog of war hung heavy over the southern states. The once peaceful fields, now scarred by the horrors of battle, were the stage for the invading army of Russian and Chinese forces, their eyes set on conquering the heartland of America. But the resilient spirit of the South was not easily subdued.

The invasion began with the precision of a well-oiled machine. Russian tanks rumbled through the fields, their tracks grinding the earth beneath them, while Chinese infantry advanced in disciplined formations, their ranks unwavering. The cities of Jackson, Mobile, and New Orleans found themselves under siege as airstrikes and artillery barrages tore through their defenses. The invaders believed the South would fall quickly, its people too divided and unprepared to mount a significant defense.

But they had underestimated the South's resolve.

From the rolling hills of Tennessee to the swamps of Louisiana, the people of the South rose, united against the foreign threat. Farmers, hunters, and former soldiers took up arms, forming militias that attacked the invaders with guerrilla tactics. They knew the land like the backs of their hands, using the thick forests and winding rivers to their advantage. Ambushes were frequent, with small, mobile units harassing supply lines, cutting off reinforcements, and disappearing into the dense wilderness before the enemy could react.

In Meridian, Mississippi, a critical turning point was unfolding. The invaders had established a stronghold in the area, using it as a base to launch more profound attacks into the South. But a coalition of local militias and remnants of the National Guard was determined to drive them out. The town's streets became a battleground, with fierce close-quarters combat raging from house to house. The invaders, trained for conventional warfare, were unprepared for the ferocity of the local resistance. Their ranks began to falter under the relentless pressure.

Word of the resistance spread like wildfire. Long proud of their independence, Southern states put aside old rivalries and came together. Volunteers flooded the front lines from Texas to Georgia, bringing a fierce determination to protect their homeland. Once confident in their superiority, the invaders now found themselves overwhelmed by their adversaries' sheer numbers and tenacity.

The final blow came at the Battle of the Bayou outside New Orleans. Russian and Chinese forces, attempting to regroup and launch a counteroffensive, were met with an all-out assault by a combined force of local militias, National Guard units, and regular Army troops. The battle was brutal and chaotic, with the dense bayou landscape providing cover for the Southern fighters. Ultimately, the invaders were trapped, their supply lines severed, and their forces encircled.

Under the cover of night, what remained of the Russian and Chinese troops began a desperate retreat. Exhausted and demoralized, they fled back the way they had come, leaving behind their dead and their equipment. The Southern forces, though battered, stood victorious, their homeland defended by the blood and sweat of its people.

The retreat marked a turning point in the broader conflict. The failed invasion of the South became a rallying cry for the rest of the nation, a symbol of resistance and resilience in the face of overwhelming odds. The South had held the line and, in doing so, had changed the course of the war.

The fog of war lifted, revealing a land scarred but unbroken. The Southern states had weathered the storm, their spirit as enduring as the oaks that dotted their fields. The invaders had been repelled, and though the road to peace would be long and hard, the South would never again be underestimated.

From the hills of Kentucky to the red clay of Alabama, the invading army felt the full force of Southern pride. The rugged terrain of the Appalachians became a natural fortress, with every ridge and valley turned into a defensive position by determined locals. In Kentucky, the invaders faced relentless ambushes from militia groups who knew the mountains like the backs of their hands. The rocky slopes and dense forests became a nightmare for the advancing troops, who found themselves constantly under attack from unseen enemies.

Further south, in Alabama, the red clay soil was stained with the blood of those who dared to cross it. The towns and farmlands of the state, steeped in a deep sense of history and tradition, became the heart of the resistance. The people of Alabama, fiercely protective of their land, took up arms with a ferocity that caught the invaders off guard. Every inch of ground was contested, and every road and bridge was a potential trap. Once confident in their superiority, the invaders were bogged down in a war of attrition, their forces stretched thin across a hostile landscape.

The spirit of Southern pride was palpable in the small towns and rural communities that dotted the region. Men and women, young and old, joined the fight, driven by a deep sense of duty to protect their homeland. They fought not just for survival but for preserving a way of life, a culture rooted in the land and history of the South. Despite their technological advantages and superior numbers, the invaders found themselves outmatched by their adversaries' sheer determination and resolve.

As the days turned into weeks, the invading army began to realize the futility of their campaign. The Southern states, united by a common cause, had become an impenetrable fortress. From the hills of Kentucky to the red clay of Alabama, the invaders were met with a force they could not overcome—a force born of pride, tradition, and unyielding love for the land they called home.

The Carbon Hill Marauders

In the dense woodlands surrounding Carbon Hill, Alabama, sharpshooters emerged as one of the most feared forces in the Southern resistance. Led by Dewey Myers, a wiry, sharp-eyed man with a knack for marksmanship, these hillbilly sharpshooters became the bane of the invading army, striking with deadly precision and then vanishing into the wilderness like ghosts.

Dewey Myers was a man of few words but many talents. Born and raised in the hills of Alabama, he had spent his entire life hunting in the region's thick forests and rugged terrain. His knowledge of the land was second to none, and his skill with a rifle was legendary. He could hit a target at distances that seemed impossible to most, and his reputation as a crack shot had earned him the respect of everyone in Carbon Hill.

When the invaders marched into Alabama, Dewey knew it was time to test his skills. Gathering a group of like-minded men, all of whom had grown up hunting and tracking in the wilds of Alabama, Dewey formed a unit of sharpshooters whose sole mission was to disrupt and demoralize the enemy. These men were not soldiers in the traditional sense; they were hunters, trappers, and farmers, but their intimate knowledge of the land and their marksmanship made them a formidable force.

The sharpshooters struck with surgical precision. They would find high ground, often in dense forests or on ridges overlooking key roads and supply lines and wait patiently for their targets. Dewey would signal when the invaders passed below, and the sharpshooters would open fire. Their aim was deadly, picking off officers, scouts, and key personnel with each shot. The invaders, caught in a lethal crossfire, would panic, often abandoning their positions in chaos.

Dewey's men specialized in hit-and-run tactics. They would strike quickly, inflicting maximum damage, and then melt back into the woods before the enemy could mount a counterattack. Unaccustomed to such guerilla warfare, the invaders found themselves at a loss. They could never predict where Dewey and his sharpshooters would strike next, and the psychological toll began to wear on them. Fear spread through their ranks as stories of the ghostly marksmen from Carbon Hill circulated among the troops.

One of Dewey's most famous exploits occurred near Jasper, where the invaders used a pivotal bridge to move troops and supplies. Hidden in the trees on either side of the river, Dewey and his men waited until a large convoy was halfway across. Then, in a coordinated attack, they opened fire, targeting the drivers of the lead and rear vehicles. The convoy came to a sudden halt, trapped on the bridge, as the sharpshooters methodically picked off the soldiers trying to take cover. By the time reinforcements arrived, the bridge was a smoking ruin, and the invaders had suffered heavy casualties.

Dewey Myers and his hillbilly sharpshooters became legends in Alabama. Their hit-and-run tactics disrupted the invaders' plans, slowed their advance, and sapped their morale. The men of Carbon Hill fought not just for their homes but for the freedom of the South, and under Dewey's leadership, they became a symbol of Southern defiance.

The invaders eventually began to avoid certain areas, knowing that Dewey and his men could be lying in wait. But no matter how far they retreated, the sharpshooters were never far behind, always ready to strike again. Dewey Myers had turned the forests and hills of Alabama into a deadly hunting ground, and the invaders, once so confident in their conquest, now found themselves hunted by the very people they had sought to subdue.

After two years of brutal warfare, the nation that had once spanned from sea to shining sea found itself irrevocably altered. The war had left deep scars on the landscape, the people, and the very fabric of what was once the United States. When the final shots were fired and the dust began to settle, the reality of the new world order became clear: America was now a divided nation.

The newly established American government, formed out of the resistance in the South and Middle America, governed 30 states. These states, united by their shared struggle and resilience, became the heart of a new nation. The ideals that had once defined America—freedom, self-reliance, and democracy—were preserved in this new American Republic, albeit within a smaller territory.

This New America was a place of pride and purpose. From the Appalachian Mountains to the Great Plains, the people who had fought so hard to defend their land turned their efforts into rebuilding. The 30 states that remained under American control were a mix of the old and the new, blending the traditions of the South with the frontier spirit of the Midwest. The government, reflecting the values that had emerged from the conflict, emphasized local governance, economic self-sufficiency, and a strong national defense to prevent future invasions.

However, the victory came at a steep cost. The other 20 states—once integral parts of the United States—were now controlled by foreign powers. Having managed to hold onto their territorial gains in the northeast and west, Russia, China, and North Korea established puppet regimes in these regions. The American people in these occupied territories lived under strict foreign rule, their freedoms curtailed, and their futures uncertain. The cities of New York, Seattle, and San Francisco, among others, were now symbols of a divided nation, their once bright futures dimmed by the shadow of foreign occupation.

The American government in the remaining 30 states refused to recognize the legitimacy of these occupations, maintaining that these lands were still American and would one day be liberated. This sentiment resonated deeply with the people of New America, who saw themselves as the bearers of the true American spirit.

Despite the division, New America had a sense of cautious optimism. The war had united the people of these 30 states in ways that had not been seen in generations. Regional differences, once a source of division, were now celebrated as part of the rich tapestry of the new nation. While more minor in the territory, the government was more decisive in unity, with leaders who had proven themselves on the battlefield now guiding the country through the arduous rebuilding process.

Internationally, New America found itself in a complex geopolitical landscape. The world had watched the war unfold with bated breath, and now, the outcome reshaped the global order. New America, determined to preserve its sovereignty and protect its people, formed alliances with other nations that shared its values, seeking to counterbalance the influence of the foreign powers that controlled the occupied territories. The United Nations, once a forum for global cooperation, was now a stage for a new Cold War, with New America and its allies on one side and the axis of Russia, China, and North Korea on the other.

Reconstruction in New America was an immense challenge. Cities devastated by the war were slowly rebuilt, and the shattered economy was gradually restored. The agricultural heartland of the Midwest became the backbone of the new economy. At the same time, the South, with its rich cultural heritage and industrial capacity, played a key role in the nation's revival.

The new government prioritized education, infrastructure, and healthcare ensuring the sacrifices made during the war would not be in vain. A new generation of Americans grew up in a smaller country but, in many ways, stronger and more cohesive than the one that had existed before the war. They were taught the history of the conflict, the importance of freedom, and the need to remain vigilant in the face of external threats.

As the years passed, New America solidified its place in the world. Though it remained a divided nation, the people of the 30 states never lost hope that the occupied territories would be free again. Memorials were built to honour those who had fallen during the war, and each year, on the anniversary of the conflict's end, the nation paused to remember the cost of their hard-won freedom.

The division of America into two distinct entities was a harsh reality, but it also represented a new beginning. Though fewer in number, the 30 states of New America were bound by a common cause and a shared destiny. They had faced the darkness of invasion and emerged into the light of a new era in which the ideals of freedom and democracy continued to shine, even in the face of adversity. The dream of a reunited America lived on, and in the people's hearts, there remained an unshakable belief that the nation would be whole again one day.

CONCLUSION

The war that had ravaged the land and tested the very soul of America finally came to an end. It had been a time of unimaginable hardship, a battle for survival against overwhelming odds. Yet, through the darkness and despair, a new light began to emerge—a light that spoke of hope, resilience, and the unbreakable spirit of a people united by a common cause.

The landscape of the nation had changed. Where once fifty states stood as one, now there were thirty, bound together by the blood, sweat, and tears of those who had fought to protect them. These thirty states, now forming the heart of New America, stood tall as a testament to the strength and determination of their people. Though smaller, this New America was vast in spirit, forged in the fires of conflict and tempered by the resolve to never again bow to tyranny.

The war had taken much from the people—loved ones, homes, and a sense of security—but it had also given them something invaluable: a renewed sense of purpose. The citizens of New America knew that their fight had not been in vain. They had preserved the ideals of freedom, democracy, and justice, ensuring that these principles would continue to guide their future.

As the nation began the process of rebuilding, there was a sense of pride in what had been accomplished. From the smallest towns to the largest cities, communities came together with a shared vision of what New America could be. The scars of war were deep but were also a reminder of what had been overcome. In every brick laid, every road repaired, and every school reopened, there was a sense of renewal and rebirth.

The leaders of New America, who had risen from the ranks of ordinary citizens to guide the nation through its darkest days, now faced the challenge of shaping its future. They understood that the strength of New America lay not in its size but in its people—the farmers of the

Midwest, the laborers of the South, and the innovators and educators who would drive the nation forward. They were determined to build a society where the sacrifices of the past would not be forgotten and where the lessons of the war would inform a future of peace and prosperity.

Internationally, New America was a hope for those still living under foreign occupation. The 20 states now controlled by Russia, China, and North Korea remained a source of deep sorrow but also of unyielding resolve. The dream of a reunited America, whole and free, lived on in the hearts of New America's citizens. They knew that one day, the flag of freedom would fly again over every inch of the land, from coast to coast.

New America blossomed into a vibrant and thriving nation in the following years. Its economy, once crippled by war, became a model of innovation and resilience. Its culture, enriched by the diverse traditions of its regions, flourished in ways that celebrated both individuality and unity. The scars of the past remained, but they were a part of the nation's story—a story of a people who, when faced with the greatest of challenges, found within themselves the strength to persevere and the courage to rebuild.

And so, as New America looked to the future, there was a deep and abiding faith in what lay ahead. The trials of the war had tested the nation's mettle, but they had also revealed its true character. New America was a land of survivors, dreamers, and doers—where freedom was not just a word but a way of life, earned through sacrifice and cherished by all.

In the end, the story of New America was one of triumph. It was a story of a nation reborn from the ashes of conflict, stronger and more united than ever. It was a story of a people who, despite the odds, refused to give up on the ideals that had defined their nation from the beginning. And as the sun rose on this new dawn, it illuminated a land filled with hope, determination, and the promise of a brighter tomorrow—a land where the spirit of America would forever endure.

About the Author

William has been a minister for 42 years. He has served congregations in Virginia, Tennssee, Indiana, California, North Dakota, and Ohio. He holds 4 undergraduate degrees and three graduate degrees. He has authored several books, and views his wife, Brenda, as his greatest supporter.

Read more at pauldingchurchofchrist.com.

www.ingramcontent.com/pod-product-compliance
Lightning Source LLC
Chambersburg PA
CBHW051906130726
47987CB00002B/995